Deception

Jess rolled her eyes. "Give me a break, Lisa. You know *exactly* what you were doing."

Lisa thought for a moment and then shook her head. "Listen, Jess, if you're so certain about this, would you please tell me? Because I still don't have a clue."

"I'm talking about Reed," Jess said.

"*Reed?*" Lisa scowled. "What about him?"

"*You* and Reed," Jess said.

"*Me* and Reed? What did we do?"

Jess stared at her for a moment, then shook her head and started walking toward the bus stop.

Other Books by Todd Strasser:

Lifeguards

SUMMER'S END

TODD STRASSER

SCHOLASTIC INC.
New York Toronto London Auckland Sydney

No part of this publication may be reproduced in whole or in part, or stored in a retrieval system, or transmitted in any form or by any means, electronic, mechanical, photocopying, recording, or otherwise, without written permission of the publisher. For information regarding permission, write to Scholastic Inc., 730 Broadway, New York, NY 10003.

ISBN 0-590-46967-3

Copyright © 1993 by Todd Strasser. All rights reserved. Published by Scholastic Inc. POINT® is a registered trademark of Scholastic Inc.

12 11 10 9 8 7 6 5 4 3 2 1   3 4 5 6 7 8/9

Printed in the U.S.A.   01

First Scholastic printing, August 1993

For Dr. Margaret Herzog, who understands.

ONE

Jess Sloat stood in front of the mirror and stared at herself in black and white. Black jeans and a black blazer over a plain white T-shirt. Her long, sun-bleached hair hung limp and lifeless over her shoulders, and despite half a summer's worth of daily sun, her skin looked pale. She wore no makeup, and the skin around her blue eyes was puffy from crying. She could hardly move. It felt as if her feet were cemented to the floor.

Gary Pilot was dead.

Gary, her friend and enemy. The determined kid who could argue forever about why he shouldn't be stopped from boogie boarding in dangerous water. The funny kid who could make her laugh in spite of herself. The kid who loved boogie boarding so much that you couldn't blame him for wanting to surf the biggest waves he could find no matter how dangerous they were.

1

Gary had drowned.

It happened the night of the big beach party at the Sandy Dunes Motel. Jess had been there . . . with Reed. She had seen Gary go boogie boarding in the rough night waters with his friends. She could have stopped him. She *would have stopped him* . . . if it hadn't been for Reed. If she hadn't been distracted by him. If she hadn't been caught up in her completely unrealistic feelings and dreams about him.

Somehow Jess had managed to forget that Reed Petersen was accustomed to a different life style than the one she was used to. He was a rich, handsome, and sophisticated guy from the city. And, he would be going away to St. Peter's prep school in a month. Jess had ignored those things. She'd let herself be blinded by stupid and impossible feelings for him.

Maybe, if he'd simply dumped her and left, she would have been better off. She could have told herself that she deserved it. She would have accepted the fact that she'd been foolish, then licked her wounds and gone ahead with her life in Far Hampton. But Reed had done something much worse than dump her. He had made her forget the things that were important — her friends, her town, and the people she was supposed to protect as a lifeguard.

And then the worst possible thing had happened. Gary Pilot had drowned right under her nose. She'd been there at the beach. She could have stopped him. . . .

If it hadn't been for Reed.

That was three days ago, and she hadn't slept more than four hours a night since. She'd hardly eaten or left her house, because she never knew when she might burst into tears. She seemed to alternate between uncontrollable crying, numbness, and disbelief. Each night she lay in bed praying that in the morning she'd wake up to discover it was all a bad dream. But it had become obvious that wasn't going to happen.

"Jess," she heard her father call from the front of the house. "Andy's here."

Jess stood in front of the mirror. She didn't answer or move. She'd been dreading this moment.

"Jess?" her father called again. "You're going to be late for the funeral."

The funeral . . .

How could she go? How could she face all of them?

Behind her, the door to her room opened. In the mirror, Jess watched her father step into the room. He was wearing jeans and a gray T-shirt. Ed Sloat was the town's police chief, but today he wasn't going into work until the afternoon.

"Hon?" he said softly.

Jess shook her head. "I can't, Dad."

Her father closed the door behind him and came a little closer. "I know you feel responsible for what happened, Jess. But I've told you that no one else feels that way. It was night. You weren't on duty. It wasn't even the beach you work at."

Jess turned and looked back at him. "If you were in another town on your day off and you saw someone being robbed, would you just walk away because it wasn't your town and you weren't on duty?"

"It's different, Jess," her father said.

"How?"

"If I stop a robbery in another town it's because an innocent person is being victimized," Chief Sloat said. "Nobody was victimizing Gary Pilot. He knew he wasn't supposed to be boogie boarding at night."

"No," Jess disagreed. "Gary never knew when he wasn't supposed to go boogie boarding. Boogie boarding was his life. He had to do it every day and everywhere. Gary would have surfed in a hurricane. It was up to me to stop him."

"You're wrong to blame yourself for this,"

her father said. "You have to believe me, Jess."

Before Jess could respond, the door behind her father opened and Andy Moncure came in. He was wearing a navy-blue blazer, a white shirt, and a striped tie. His dark hair was slicked down. Jess couldn't help noticing that he'd started to grow it long. Like Reed's. And his clothes had gotten preppy. Like Reed's.

"Uh, sorry, I didn't mean to interrupt," he said a little nervously as he glanced from Jess to her father. "Uh, hi, Chief Sloat."

"Hi, Andy," Jess's father said. "It's all right. Jess and I were just talking."

"Well, we really should go, Jess," Andy said. "Or we're gonna be late."

Jess nodded slowly. She knew they were right. She had to go. Thank God she had her father and Andy. They'd both been so supportive. Especially Andy. After all, he knew she'd been with Reed the night Gary drowned. Jess wouldn't have blamed him if he'd totally given up on her after what she'd done. Instead he was still there for her. Completely. Even when she called him in the middle of the night in tears. He stayed on the phone with her for hours.

How could she ever have forgotten what Andy meant to her? How could she ever have taken his friendship for granted? Or been so stupid as to risk losing it? Jess crossed the room toward him. Short and solidly built, Andy had always been the pillar she leaned on.

"I'll see you later, Dad," she said.

"Uh, Jess," her father said, sliding his hand into his back pocket and taking out a worn brown leather wallet. He took out a twenty-dollar bill and handed it to her. "After the funeral, why don't you and Andy go get something to eat. Your mother says you've hardly eaten and you haven't left the house for days. It would be good for you to get out and eat some junk food."

"Thanks, Dad." Jess gave him a kiss on the cheek and then left.

It was a hot sunny day. Jess squinted in the sunlight as she left the house. A sense of surprise ran through her, as if she'd forgotten it was the middle of the summer. As they went down the walk, she slipped her hand into Andy's. He gave her a questioning look, but seemed to understand that she needed to feel his support.

"Your old man must be really worried about you," Andy said as they walked toward his mother's car, a beat-up green Buick with a cracked windshield. It was a Far Hampton kind of car. At least for the locals.

"Why?" Jess asked absently.

"Why?" Andy repeated, surprised. "Because he gave you twenty bucks and told you to go eat junk food after the funeral. You ever remember him doing anything like that before?"

Jess shrugged.

"I know you're not ready for the funeral," Andy said as he got into the driver's seat and gave her a concerned look. "Are you sure you want to do this?"

"As long as you stay with me, Andy."

"Hey." Andy gave her an encouraging smile. "Don't worry, I'll be with you all the way."

The car had no air conditioning. As Andy drove, Jess rolled down the window and let the hot air blow in. She could feel the heat of the sun being absorbed by the black material covering her arms and legs.

"Reed's going to be there, you know," Andy said, glancing over at her as he drove toward town.

Jess nodded.

"You sure you can handle that?"

"No," Jess answered, "but it doesn't look like I have a choice."

"Yes, you do. We don't have to go."

"How can I not go?"

"Easy, Jess. We'll just go to McDonald's."

"You know I can't do that," Jess said. "I have to go. I owe it to Gary."

Andy nodded, but didn't reply. Jess assumed he wasn't happy about her seeing Reed. The truth was, he shouldn't have worried about it. Seeing Reed was the last thing in the world she wanted to do. If she'd learned one thing from this terrible experience, it was that she was a lot better off without Reed Petersen in her life.

"Have you . . ." Andy began and then shook his head. "No, forget it."

"What, Andy?"

"I was going to ask if you'd spoken to him since it happened, but it's none of my business."

It might not have been any of his business, but Jess could tell he was dying to know.

"He called a few times, but I told him I had nothing to say," she said. "One night he even came by in his jeep, but I told Mom to tell him I had a headache."

"Do you think you'll talk to him again at some point?" Andy asked.

Jess turned and gazed out the window. "I don't think I can," she said.

For the funeral, Lisa Jones had chosen to wear a plain black dress and her faded denim jacket with a rose on its back. Cut in a pageboy, her short black hair fell straight down the sides of her head, and she wore no makeup.

As a rookie lifeguard, Lisa had met Gary Pilot at the beach. Gary was five years younger than she. Like most of her friends, Lisa was shocked that anyone so young could actually die.

At the church before the funeral began, Lisa and Ellie Sax, a fifth-year lifeguard, stood apart from the crowd of people waiting on the steps to go inside.

"Aren't you hot in that jacket?" Ellie asked. As usual, her hair was in a thick brown braid down the middle of her back. Like Lisa, she wore a plain black dress.

"Yes," Lisa said, "but I always wear it. It's like my security blanket. I'd wear it in the lifeguard chair if Hank let me."

"Have you seen Hank yet?" Ellie asked.

"He went inside before with Reed," Lisa said.

"What about Jess?"

"I haven't seen her," Lisa said. "When I talked to her yesterday, she wasn't sure she was coming."

Ellie nodded. "She hasn't come to the beach since it happened. She's lucky Hank's so understanding."

"She's really taking it hard," Lisa said. "Not

just because she knew Gary. But because she blames herself for not stopping him that night."

"You know who she was with, don't you?" Ellie said.

"Reed," Lisa said. It was common knowledge.

"Reed told me she won't talk to him," Ellie said quietly. "It's almost like she blames him for distracting her."

A beat-up green Buick turned the corner and Lisa saw Andy and Jess inside. Lisa wasn't surprised they'd come together. She knew that if Jess came to the funeral, she'd have to come with Andy. Ever since Gary had drowned, Andy had stuck to Jess like glue. If Lisa had been different, she might have thought Andy was using Gary's death as an excuse to get close to Jess again. But Lisa wasn't like that — she knew that Andy had reached out to Jess because they were old friends. And at a time like this you needed an old friend. Someone you could be honest with, someone you could let down your defenses with. For Lisa, it was a poignant feeling because she was new in town and had no one she really felt close to.

Except Jess . . . and Andy. . . .

Not that she felt that close to him yet. But she liked him and hoped that someday she *could* be close to him. If only he'd give her the chance. For a while, when it seemed that Jess was going

to get together with Reed Petersen, Lisa thought
that Andy had finally given up on his secret
crush. But then Gary had drowned and everything had changed.

Lisa watched Andy turn the car down the side
street that led to the church parking lot. She
couldn't help wondering if it was over between
Jess and Reed. Because if it was, Jess might someday go from being Andy's best friend to being
his girlfriend. And Lisa would be left behind.

Stop thinking like that! Lisa scolded herself.
Now was the time to be supportive. Right now
they all needed each other.

Parked cars lined the street in front of the Pres-
byterian church. Andy couldn't help noticing
Reed's gun-metal-gray jeep among them. So
Reed was there. Andy knew that Jess claimed
she never wanted to see Reed again and he believed her. But . . . Reed was the kind of guy
who could change a girl's mind. Andy had seen
it happen before. He knew it could happen again.

Andy drove around to the asphalt lot behind
the church and parked.

"Ready?" he asked, looking across the seat at
Jess.

Jess stared out the window and didn't answer.

"Jess?"

Jess took a deep breath and nodded.

"We really don't have to go in," Andy said. "I'm sure people would understand that you were too upset."

"I have to go," Jess said and pushed open the car door.

They got out and started to walk down the sidewalk. The sun was a little higher now, and the air outside felt a little hotter. As they approached the church steps, Andy saw Lisa Jones come toward them.

"Hi, Andy," Lisa said.

"Hi, Lisa." Andy felt awkward. He had not treated Lisa very nicely lately.

Lisa turned to Jess and hugged her. "How are you?"

Jess answered with a shrug. Lisa stared up at her.

"You sure you're going to be okay with this?"

"No," Jess replied. "But I have to be here."

"I know." Lisa slid her arm around Jess's waist. Together with Andy they walked toward the church.

The church was hot and crowded. In one way or another, Gary Pilot had touched the lives of many people and now they were all here to mourn him. The pews in the front were filled with Gary's friends, all kids in their early teens with chopped haircuts and earrings. In the row just behind them sat Reed Petersen in a dark suit. Next to him was Hank Diamond, the sandy-haired lifeguard captain at Far Hampton public beach.

In front of the pews and before the altar was a dark mahogany casket covered with yellow flowers. Gary's chipped, scratched, yellow-and-black boogie board was propped up beside it, along with a large color photo of Gary in his tattered pink-and-black wetsuit, a big grin on his face.

"Hard to believe he's gone," Hank muttered.

Reed nodded. Like the other lifeguards, he'd had plenty of run-ins with Gary over where he was allowed to surf. Like the rest, he had come to appreciate the charming, argumentative kid. And like Jess, he felt responsible for Gary's drowning. He'd been at the beach that night. Even though he'd had no authority at the time, he should have warned Gary that boogie board-ing in the dark was dangerous.

Reed hung his head and stared at the floor. "I should have stopped him, Hank."

"You can't be everyone's guardian angel, Reed," Hank replied.

"I could have said something," Reed said.

"Listen, Reed, I've worked the beach for more than fifteen years," Hank said. "I've seen a lot of good lifeguards come and go, but I've never known anyone who worked harder or was more dedicated than you. Sandy Dunes wasn't your beach, you weren't on duty, and you had other things on your mind. What happened to Gary was a terrible accident, Reed, but it wasn't your fault."

Reed nodded. He'd heard all this before, but it didn't change the fact that he could have done something to prevent Gary from drowning.

Reed stared at the large color photograph of Gary and then slowly turned to look at the open doors at the back of the church. He was wondering where Jess was. Perhaps he wasn't supposed to be thinking of her at that moment, but he couldn't help himself. He'd called her several times since Gary drowned, but it seemed as if she didn't want to speak to him.

He'd heard from the other lifeguards that she'd taken Gary's death very hard. That like Reed, she blamed herself because she was at the beach that night and could have stopped Gary. But Reed suspected there was more to the story. . . . Although none of his friends would say so, he had a feeling Jess was blaming *him* for Gary's death as well.

Three figures appeared in the doorway of the church. Reed recognized them at once: Jess, Andy Moncure, and Lisa Jones. He watched as Jess stepped into the church, her eyes cast downward. Was she afraid he'd be there? Was she afraid to make eye contact? Reed felt the sudden urge to get up and go to her, but he fought it. Despite what he felt, this wasn't the right time or place.

But he couldn't take his eyes off her. This was the first time he'd seen her in days. As he stared at her long, willowy beauty, he felt a deep yearning inside. He missed her badly. It was hard not to think back to that night on the beach when they lay in each others arms . . . the softness of her lips against his . . . the smell of her hair and the warmth of her skin . . . they were haunting memories now, moments he couldn't forget.

Andy held Jess's arm tightly as they entered the church. He was worried this might be too much for her. He felt her hesitate as the crowd's eyes turned to look at her. He heard her gasp as Gary's casket came into view.

They found an empty pew about halfway down the aisle and filed into it. By now most of the faces had turned back toward the front, but one remained watching them. Andy recognized

Reed and gave him a curt nod. Reed didn't nod back. Andy would have liked to think that it was because Reed was a snob, but he knew that wasn't the reason. The reason Reed hadn't nodded back was because he wasn't looking at Andy. He was looking at Jess.

Andy, Lisa, and Jess sat down in the pew with Andy still holding Jess tightly. It wasn't hard to guess what Reed was thinking. He still wanted Jess by his side to show off to his prep school buddies from the city. After all, what was cooler than having the hottest babe on the beach? To Reed, Jess was just another toy. Like his jeep and his sailboat and whatever else he had stuffed away in that mansion he lived in.

Well, Andy had almost allowed Reed to have Jess before. In fact, for Jess's sake, he'd almost tried to make sure it happened. But that was then and this was now. He wasn't going to make the same mistake twice.

The church grew quiet as the minister came out to the pulpit and began the funeral service. For the next half hour, they all forgot about their own concerns and focused only on the minister's words and on their memories of Gary.

Because it was such a hot day, the doors of the church were left open. No one noticed that one more person arrived during the service. Wearing sunglasses and dark clothes, he slipped inside the church and stood in the shadows just inside the doorway.

Billy Petersen had not come to mourn Gary Pilot. To him Gary was just a goofy kid who should have known better than to go boogie boarding at night. To Billy, Gary's drowning was one of the least important things that had happened the night of the party at the Sandy Dunes Motel. More important, Jess Sloat had tricked him into confessing that he'd stolen a Doppler radar, an expensive piece of equipment, from the lifeguard shack, and that he'd hidden it on his brother's sailboat so Reed would get into trouble. And even though Billy had found Jess's hidden tape recorder and gotten rid of the evidence, the truth had come out.

In the days that had followed, Billy had been put through the wringer. The town had dropped theft charges against one brother and brought them instead against the other. In his defense, Billy showed the letter Reed had sent to Hank to get him demoted from senior lifeguard. But Reed denied ever writing the letter and of course everyone believed him.

Finally Billy's father made a deal with Hank and Police Chief Sloat. Billy was thrown off the

lifeguard crew for good. He had to do six hours
of community service a day for the rest of the
summer, *and* he had a nine o'clock curfew on
weekday nights and a ten o'clock curfew on the
weekends. Mr. Petersen also made a large do-
nation to the town's recreation fund.

Once again Reed had come out the win-
ner . . . for now. But more than ever, Billy was
determined not to let it stay that way.

As the minister spoke, Billy gazed around the
church. He spotted his brother sitting with
Hank, and he saw Jess sitting with Andy Moncure and Lisa Jones. Then he noticed someone
sitting alone in the far corner of the last pew.
She was wearing a black dress and black stock-
ings and her face was hidden beneath a black
veil. But the way she chewed gum was unmis-
takable. Billy smiled to himself. So Paula was
here, too.

TWO

The service ended with a prayer. Then a man in a suit walked up the aisle asking for pallbearers to carry the casket. Several people quickly volunteered, but they were still one man short. Jess saw Reed Petersen start to raise his hand. Beside her, Andy quickly jumped up and volunteered first.

"Where are you going?" Jess whispered.

"Gary Pilot was born in Far Hampton and grew up here," Andy replied. "There's no way a city kid like Reed Petersen is going to help carry his casket."

Andy slid out of the pew and joined the other guys gathering around the casket. Lisa slid closer to Jess.

"I guess he really means it," she said.

Jess nodded, but she felt uncomfortable and vulnerable without Andy nearby. It was the first time she'd ventured out into the world since

Gary drowned and she felt as if she needed protection.

A few moments later, Andy and the other guys passed, carrying the casket. A sobbing woman and grim-looking man followed, and Jess realized they must have been Gary's parents. God, she felt awful. She just wanted to throw herself at their feet and beg for forgiveness. Then the rest of the congregation followed as the pew in front of Jess and Lisa emptied.

"Shouldn't we go?" Lisa whispered in Jess's ear.

But Jess felt frozen in her seat, unable to join the crowd of mourners following the casket out.

"Jess?" Lisa whispered.

"You go," Jess whispered back.

"And leave you?"

Jess nodded.

"Why? What's wrong?"

Before Jess could answer, she felt Reed's penetrating dark eyes on her. She knew that he'd be passing her pew on his way out. Hank and Ellie were with him. As they reached the pew where Jess and Lisa sat, Hank paused.

"Jess, Lisa, you want to ride to the cemetery with us?"

Jess couldn't answer. She couldn't even look

at the lifeguard captain. She just stared down at the floor.

Lisa looked up at Hank and shook her head. "Thanks, but I think we'll wait."

"All right," Hank said. "We'll see you later."

Hank and Ellie joined the crowd again, but Reed stood at the end of the pew. "Jess?" he said.

Jess closed her eyes and shook her head. She heard Lisa tell Reed, "It's not a good time."

Jess kept her eyes closed a moment more.

"He went," Lisa said.

Jess opened her eyes and let out a long breath. Reed was gone, but she still wanted to wait.

A few minutes later the church was empty except for someone wearing a veil in the far corner of the last pew.

"You okay?" Lisa asked Jess.

"No, but I'll survive," Jess replied. "And thanks for staying with me. You saved my life."

"Just think," Lisa said. "My first rescue and I didn't even have to go in the water."

Jess gave her a crooked smile.

"Do you want to go now?" Lisa asked.

"I guess." Jess started to get up.

They walked up the aisle and stepped out of the church. The sun was even brighter than before, and Jess had to squint. On the street in front of the church, the hearse carrying the casket pulled away, followed by several long black limousines. Everyone else was walking toward their cars to drive to the cemetery. Still squinting, Jess looked around for Andy.

"He went in one of the limos," a voice said.

Jess felt a shiver. It was Reed's voice. He was sitting in his jeep, double-parked in front of the church. He looked handsome in his suit with his longish chestnut-brown hair combed low over his forehead.

"But he drove me here," Jess replied, caught off guard.

"I guess they wanted to make sure all the pall-bearers got to the cemetery at the same time," Reed replied. "Can I give you a ride?"

"Uh, thanks," Jess said quickly, "but I think I'll go with Lisa."

"Uh, we can't." Lisa bit her lips. "My car died. My father dropped me off here. I was going to try to find a ride to the cemetery myself."

"I promise I won't bite," Reed said.

Jess had been dreading something like this. The last thing in the world she wanted to do was to be with Reed. She looked desperately for someone else to catch a ride with, but she recognized no one. Meanwhile, Reed hadn't moved.

"What's wrong?" Lisa whispered to her.

Jess couldn't explain it there on the church steps with Reed barely thirty feet away. Instead she mustered her strength and started down toward the street.

Reed leaned over and pushed open the passenger door. Jess climbed in first and sat in the back. Lisa got into the front passenger seat and closed the door.

"Everyone wearing seat belts?" Reed asked, glancing at Jess in the rearview mirror. Jess nodded and strapped hers on.

"You're not taking any chances, are you?" Lisa said to Reed.

"Not after what happened," Reed replied soberly.

No one spoke during the ride to the cemetery. In the front seat Lisa's short black hair fluttered in the wind. In the back seat, where it was even windier, Jess twisted her long blonde hair into a ponytail and tried to tuck it under the collar of her black blazer. A white St. Peter's Prep baseball cap was lying on the backseat, but Jess couldn't bring herself to put it on.

Several times she noticed Reed glancing at her

in the rearview mirror. It reminded her of a night not long ago when she'd sat in the back of the jeep as Reed drove along the beach with his brother, Billy, in front. That night Reed hadn't been able to take his eyes off her and he'd almost run into a log lying on the sand.

More memories of the electric feelings she'd felt toward him came back . . . powerful feelings and sensations she'd never felt for anyone before. Only a week ago they'd thrilled her. Now they were frightening.

They arrived at the cemetery. Reed parked the jeep and got out. He stood beside the car waiting for Lisa and Jess.

"Lisa," he said, "would you mind if I spoke to Jess alone for a moment?"

Jess stared helplessly at her friend, wishing Lisa would do something outrageous like shout, "Yes!" But she knew she wouldn't. Instead, Lisa only nodded and started walking toward the crowd gathering around the grave site.

Jess felt her heart start to pound anxiously. She wished she could just run away. Far away from all the memories of Reed and Gary and the whole first half of that summer.

"How are you, Jess?" Reed asked, gazing intensely at her with those dark eyes.

"Okay, I guess." Jess shrugged and looked away at the rows of tombstones covering the sloping hill behind them.

"Look, I know I can't take much time," Reed said. "You've been avoiding me and I have a feeling I know why. But I'd really like to talk to you. I *have* to talk to you. Just promise me that you won't keep avoiding me."

Jess nodded numbly.

"Can we talk after the funeral?" Reed asked.

"No!" Jess blurted out. It was too soon. She couldn't. She wasn't ready for this.

"Then tonight?" Reed asked.

Jess knew there was no point in making a million excuses and trying to postpone it. Maybe the best thing to do was get it over with.

"All right, Reed," she said. "Tonight."

"Your house?"

Ever since the drowning, Jess felt safest in her own home, but somehow it didn't feel right. It was too close. She didn't feel comfortable seeing Reed there.

"The Main chair," she said.

"See you there." Reed walked ahead toward the group around the open grave.

When the mourners left the church, Billy Petersen had stepped into a corner and stayed out of sight. But he'd kept an eye on Paula, who remained seated in the last pew in the corner. After waiting for what seemed like forever, Billy noticed that Jess and Lisa had finally left, and that the church had emptied. Billy watched Paula get up and start toward the doors. He stepped out of the shadows.

"I didn't know you were a friend of Gary Pilot's," he said just as Paula reached the doors.

He enjoyed watching her freeze and turn around.

"Billy!" she gasped.

"It's been a while, Paula," Billy said with a nasty smile. "Not since we talked at the Crab Shack, remember? When you explained so nicely how the cops wouldn't believe me if I told them you'd convinced me to steal the radar."

"What do you want?" Paula asked nervously.

"I don't know, Paula," Billy replied. "What would *you* want from someone who'd used you?"

"I didn't use you," Paula said. "We had a deal. You'd take the radar and make it seem like Reed stole it. And I'd get you Jess. It wasn't my fault if you got drunk and tried to molest her."

Billy grinned. "Is that what you heard?"

"Yes."

"Don't you want to hear my side of the story?" Billy asked.

Paula stared at him for a moment. "Not particularly," she said and then turned to go out the open church doors.

Billy quickly stepped into her path, blocking her way. "You never got me Jess," he said. "You never intended to keep your half of the deal."

"Of course I did," Paula said. She tried to dart around him, but Billy grabbed her arm.

"Let go!" she said, trying to pull her arm out of his grasp. But Billy held tight.

"It was just luck that I got together with Jess," Billy said angrily. "Lucky for you, that is, because it made it seem like you were keeping your half of the deal. The truth is the only reason Jess pretended she was interested in me was because she wanted to get me to confess I stole the radar."

Paula was still struggling to get her arm out of his grasp. "If you don't let go right now, I'll scream," she threatened.

Billy let go and Paula quickly stepped outside and started down the church steps. But Billy followed right behind her.

"You really think you can run away?" Billy called behind her. "You really think I can't find you if I want to?"

Paula got to the sidewalk and stopped. She turned to face him.

"Look, I don't know what you want, Billy," she said, pulling off the dark veil. "The plan didn't work. *Neither* of us got what we wanted. So we're even, okay?"

"Not quite," Billy said. "You're walking around free and clear. No one suspects you had anything to do with stealing the radar. Meanwhile, I lost my job as a lifeguard. I'm the one who has to be in every night by nine o'clock and spend every day picking up litter at the beach."

"Well, that's life," Paula said with a shrug. "We both took a chance. It's not my fault you got caught."

Paula started walking down the sidewalk.

"So what were you doing here, Paula?" Billy asked as he fell into step beside her.

"Nothing." Paula quickened her pace.

"You just like going to funerals?" Billy asked.

"Get off it, Billy," Paula fumed.

"Maybe you were there to spy on Reed," Billy guessed. "Maybe you wanted to see if he and Jess were still together. Maybe deep down inside you still want Reed back."

Instead of answering, Paula just started walking faster.

"Hey," Billy said with a laugh as he kept up

with her. "What are you so upset about? It looked to me like Jess wanted nothing to do with Reed."

Yes, Paula thought to herself. That was exactly what it looked like. And that was why she had to distance herself from Billy as fast as she could. She reached her car and quickly unlocked the door and pulled it open. She got into the driver's seat, but before she could slam the door, Billy grabbed it and kept it open.

"I'm not finished with you yet," he said.

"Well, I'm finished with you," Paula said, trying to pull the door closed. She wished he'd just go away and leave her alone.

"There are just a couple of other things we have to talk about," Billy said.

Paula gripped the steering wheel so angrily her knuckles turned white. "What, Billy?" she snapped impatiently.

"Well, let's see," Billy said, taking his time. Paula could see that he enjoyed making her uncomfortable.

"There's that letter Hank got," Billy said. "The one that got me demoted from senior guard. The one you said you found in the garbage can in the lifeguard shack."

"I did find it there," Paula insisted.

"You know, if it hadn't been for that letter, I probably never would have set my brother up," Billy said. "But you convinced me he was the one who wrote it."

"He was," Paula said, avoiding his eyes.

"Yeah, that's what I thought, too," Billy said. "I mean, you think I would have set my own brother up if he hadn't written that letter?"

"I don't really care what you would have done," Paula replied irritably. She tried to yank the car door closed, but Billy held it open.

"A funny thing happened when everyone found out I stole the radar," Billy said. "My old man arranged a big sit-down with the cops and Hank to decide what they were gonna do with me. So while we were all sitting there I happened to ask Hank about the letter, and you know what? He opened this folder he'd brought with him and there it was. He even let me hold it and read it."

Paula had a feeling that was what Billy had been getting at. Once again she tried to yank the door closed, but Billy stopped her and leaned closer.

"Pretty amazing, isn't it?" Billy asked. "That Hank had the letter and *you* had the letter. So if Hank never threw his out, where did you get the one you said you found in his garbage can?"

"If you don't get away from this car right now, I'm going to scream," Paula threatened him.

But Billy didn't move. "Go ahead," he dared her. "And maybe when the cops get here I'll tell them how you must've snuck into our house and written the letter on my brother's computer. And how you must've made two copies and forged my brother's signature on both. Then you sent one to Hank and kept the other to show to me. I don't know the law that well, Paula, but I have a feeling the police might decide that makes you an accessory to the crime."

Paula turned and glared at him. "All right, you want to know the truth? I *did* write that letter. But I know Reed. If I hadn't sent that letter, Reed would have. There was no way he would let you be a senior guard and goof around the way you did. You know how Reed thinks. Too many people's lives were at stake."

Billy just laughed. "That's pretty slick, Paula. You forge a letter to get me to commit a crime and then say Reed would have written the letter if you hadn't."

"Look," Paula said, "it's over now, okay? I'm really sorry you got caught. But that's life, Billy. And there's no way you're going to be able to convince anyone I wrote those letters. It's just your word against mine."

"No, Paula," Billy said with a smile. "It's your word against *you*."

Paula stared at him. "What are you talking about?"

"Didn't you hear how Jess bought a little tape recorder and tried to tape my confession the night of the party at Sandy Dunes?" Billy asked, reaching into his shirt. "Well, it gave me this great idea."

The next thing Paula knew, Billy pulled a small tape recorder out of his shirt. It was about the size of a pack of cigarettes. Billy pushed a button and it began to play. Paula heard her own voice saying, "*. . . there's no way you're going to be able to convince anyone I wrote those letters. It's just your word against mine.*"

"Why, you bastard!" Paula tried to grab the tape recorder, but Billy quickly pulled it out of her reach.

"I'll tell you, Paula," Billy said glibly as he put the tape recorder back into his pocket. "Now that I have a curfew every night, I've really gotten big time into the world of electronic surveillance."

Paula felt the blood drain out of her face. She knew she must have looked pale as a ghost. "You're not going to go to the police, are you?"

"I might," Billy replied.

"Billy, please," Paula begged. "If my father ever finds out, he'll kill me."

"I bet he would," Billy said with a smile.

"Do you want money?" Paula opened her handbag and took out her wallet.

"Nope." Billy grinned.

"Then what?" Paula asked desperately.

"You'll see soon enough."

Suddenly Paula had another thought. "You're going to give it to Reed?"

"Now that's a distinct possibility," Billy replied.

"No, don't," Paula begged. "Please. Just tell me what you want."

Instead of replying, Billy pushed the car door closed. "I'll be in touch," he said, and walked away.

THREE

The graveside service was short. The minister said a prayer and then some of the mourners threw flowers on the casket as it was lowered into the ground. After adding flowers of their own, Jess, Andy, and Lisa turned away and walked back toward the cars. Jess glanced at Reed and their eyes met briefly. He was standing beside the jeep, watching them. Jess wondered why he didn't offer them a ride this time. Was it because Reed sensed that Andy was against him?

Instead, Hank gave them a ride in his van. Andy asked him to take them back to the church where he'd left his mother's car. A little while later Hank pulled the van into the lot behind the church.

"Thanks, Hank," Andy said, sliding the van's side door open. "See you in the morning."

Jess waited in the van while Andy and Lisa

got out. Then Hank leaned over the front seat toward her.

"Got a minute?" he asked.

"Uh, okay," Jess replied. A slight shiver ran through her. She had a feeling she knew what was coming. "Just let me tell Andy and Lisa."

Jess got out of the van.

"Feel like pizza?" Andy asked.

"Why don't you go ahead and I'll catch up," Jess said as Hank got out of the van and came around.

Andy glanced at them both and scowled. "What's up?"

"Hank wants to speak to me," Jess explained.

Andy nodded. "Okay, we'll wait for you over at Villa Maria."

Jess watched Andy and Lisa walk away.

"They seem like good friends for you," Hank said.

"They are," said Jess.

"So . . ." Hank shielded his eyes from the sun. "Why don't we go sit down on the bench under the tree where there's some shade."

They walked over to the bench and sat down. It had turned out to be one of those excruciating August days. So hot that the birds stopped chirping and the bugs stopped buzzing. Hank opened the collar of his frayed white dress shirt and pulled loose the ancient foulard tie he'd chosen to wear. His jacket was too small. It had been a long time since he had had an occasion to wear a jacket and tie.

Hank was clearly uncomfortable and kept running his hand over his short blond hair.

"This is the kind of day where the only good place to be is at the beach," he said.

"Too bad neither of us is there," Jess said.

"Yeah." Hank nodded. "Actually, Jess, that's sort of what I wanted to speak to you about. I know this is a terrible time to bring it up . . . but you haven't been to work since Gary drowned and, well . . . I sort of have to know what your plans are."

"I wish I knew what my plans were," Jess said with a sigh.

Hank nodded and shoved his hands into the pockets of his baggy slacks. "I know how you must feel, Jess. That's why I hope you'll come back to work."

"I don't follow," Jess said, puzzled.

"Well, I guess it has to do with what being a good lifeguard is all about," Hank said. "It isn't just a matter of being a strong swimmer or having good eyes. It also takes someone who really cares. It's pretty obvious that you feel that way."

"Maybe," Jess said with a shrug. "But if I were really a good lifeguard, Gary Pilot would be alive today."

"I'm not sure you could have stopped Gary," Hank said. "It was night, it wasn't your beach, and you weren't on duty. Besides, Gary's friends say that you *did* try to stop him."

Jess nodded. "But later on I saw him out there in the waves with his friends."

"Well, I'll be honest, Jess. If I thought you deserved even a shred of blame, I'd tell you. But I honestly think you did the right thing and are completely blameless. You know that Gary's parents don't blame you for what happened, either. In fact, Gary's father told me he only wishes Gary had listened to you when you told him not to go into the water."

To Jess it was a small consolation considering what had happened. "I'll be honest with you, too, Hank," she said. "I'd like to come back. I really do like lifeguarding. But if something like this happened again . . ." Jess let her words trail off and just shook her head. She couldn't even talk about it.

"Like I said, Jess, I hate to have to ask this now," Hank said. "But I have to know what your plans are. If you decide to quit, I won't be happy, but I'll understand. The thing is, I have to know whether or not to hire someone new for the rest of the summer."

Jess watched a couple of kids ride by on bikes, carrying boogie boards under their arms. The beach had always been a part of her life. Even after only a few days away she missed it. It was hard for her to make any kind of decision about lifeguarding right now.

Finally she had an idea. "Can I call you tonight?" she asked. "I promise by then I'll make up my mind."

Hank rubbed his chin. "Well, I'm not certain I understand what's going to change between now and then, but sure, that's fine."

Hank walked back to his van, and Jess walked down the hot sidewalk to the pizza place. Villa Maria was just a storefront with three red booths and a small counter, but they had the best pizza in Far Hampton. And the air conditioning felt great.

"He wants to know if you're coming back to work," Andy said as Jess joined him and Lisa in a booth.

"Yup," Jess said.

"What did you tell him?" Lisa asked.

"That I'd call him tonight."

Andy took a sip of his soda. "So when are you going to talk to Reed?"

"Tonight," Jess said.

"Wow, sounds like you're going to have a busy evening," said Lisa.

"I guess." Jess wasn't looking forward to any of it.

"I still don't understand why you feel you have to talk to Reed," Andy said as he sprinkled garlic powder and oregano on his pizza.

"I just do, Andy," Jess said. "Please don't give me a hard time."

Andy let his mouth fall open and made his eyes bulge. "Vhat? Me give you a hard time?" he asked in a funny old man's voice. "Never! Vhat do you tink I am, your fadder? Forget it! And I ain't your mudder, neither."

"Andy . . ." Jess couldn't help smiling.

"Nope. Forget it!" Andy said, shaking his head. "Just because I tink Reed Petersen's a bad influence don't mean I don't feel *a bond* wit him."

"*Andy, stop* . . ." Jess was chuckling now.

"If you were talking about Billy, I'd understand," Lisa said. "But why is Reed a bad influence?"

"Vell, you know dem guys from da big city," Andy went on. "Dey go to dem fancy prop schools."

"It's *prep* schools," Jess corrected him with a laugh.

Andy threw his hand up. "Prop! Prep! Vhat's da difference!" He leaned forward and pointed his finger at Jess. "I'll tell you vhat's da difference. Dem boys from da city. Dey got different values."

"What kind of values?" Lisa giggled.

"Just look at da way dey treats people," Andy said, waving his arms. "Dem guys from da city don't tink twice about using you." Andy banged his fist on the table. "It's dat darned tissue theory of life!"

"The what?" Jess asked with a laugh.

"Da tissue theory," Andy said. "Use it once, den trow it avay. I mean, vhat does Reed have to lose? He can use you all he vants dis summer, den he'll go off to dat fancy prop school in da fall and you'll never hear from him. Maybe next summer he von't even come to Far Hampton. Maybe he'll go to Maine . . . or back to the old country!"

Jess and Lisa looked at each other and rolled their eyes.

"But suppose one of us went someplace else over the summer," Lisa said to Andy. "Does that automatically mean we'd be using anyone we met, too?"

"Ven was da last time any of us could afford to go anywhere for da summer?" Andy asked back. "I mean, I'm lucky my mudder's sending me to stay wit my cousins in New Hampshire for a week."

"I guess you've got a point there," Lisa said. "But I still don't see why Reed's relationship with Jess would be any different from his relationship with any other girl."

"*Dat's vhat I keep telling you!*" Andy said, raising his voice. "It's because we ain't like dem. Dis Reed vill fool around wit anyone, but he's gonna marry someone like him. Someone from da same kind of schools, someone wit da same kind of money. *Someone from de old country!*"

Lisa leaned forward and tapped Jess on the shoulder. "Did you know we were talking about marriage?"

Jess had to smile.

"Go ahead and smile," Andy said, returning to his normal voice. "But I think you were hurt pretty bad, and you only knew Reed for a few weeks. I don't think you'd be smiling if you went with Reed for a whole summer and then he took off and dumped you."

Jess and Lisa shared a look. The smile vanished from Jess's face, and the moment of levity was gone.

"I think maybe it's time we talked about something else," Lisa said.

*   *   *

After lunch, Andy dropped them off at Jess's house, then drove to the beach. He'd told Jess and Lisa that he had to get the car back to his mother, but he wanted to make a stop first.

Andy knew that Hank had made an arrangement for a replacement crew of lifeguards to fill in at the Far Hampton public beach while the regular lifeguard crew attended Gary Pilot's funeral. But some of the regulars were supposed to go back to work in the afternoon. Reed was one of them.

Andy drove into the beach parking lot and stopped near the lifeguard shack. Reed's jeep wasn't there yet. He'd probably gone home to change out of his suit before coming to work. Andy got out of his car, took off his jacket, and rolled up his shirt sleeves. It was very hot and the beach was crowded with people and umbrellas. A lot of the patrons were in the water today. The usual breeze off the ocean was absent. Andy wiped some sweat off his brow with the sleeve of his shirt. He was thinking he might grab a bus back to the beach later and take a swim himself.

A moment later Reed's jeep pulled into the parking lot. Wearing sunglasses, a white T-shirt, and his orange Far Hampton lifeguard trunks, Reed hopped out and started jogging toward the lifeguard shack. Typical, Andy thought. Even in this heat Reed had to be so gung ho, so much better than anyone else.

"Hey, Reed," Andy called, walking slowly toward him.

Reed was surprised when he heard Andy's voice and turned to see him crossing the parking lot, still wearing his shirt and slacks from the funeral.

"Hey, Andy, what's up?" Reed said.

"Got a second?" Andy asked.

"Well, I'm supposed to go on duty pretty soon," Reed said, "but sure, I've got a couple of seconds."

"I want to talk to you about Jess," Andy said, stopping a few feet from Reed.

Reed gave him an uncertain look. "Okay."

"You know she's in pretty bad shape over the drowning," Andy said. "She pretty much blames herself for what happened."

Reed nodded, wondering what Andy was getting at.

"She's also thinking about quitting the crew," Andy said.

"That's too bad," Reed said. "She's a good lifeguard. We need her."

"Well, she's just feeling really shaky about everything right now," Andy said. "That's why I wanted to talk to you. She told me you were going to talk to her tonight. I know I can't stop you, but I just want to ask a favor. Don't lead her on, okay?"

The implications shocked Reed. For a moment he just stared at Andy in amazement, wondering why it was any of his business. Of course, he knew Andy was jealous. But the night of the Sandy Dunes party, it had been Andy himself who'd told Reed the truth about why Jess had gone off with Billy. If it hadn't been for Andy, Reed and Jess probably never would have gotten together that night.

"Why would I lead Jess on?" Reed asked.

"Don't give me that," Andy said. "You know why."

"No. I don't," Reed said.

Andy stepped closer. "Let me tell you something, Reed. You remember the night of the Sandy Dunes party? I told you the truth about Jess because I care about her and I didn't want to see her get hurt. The thing is, I had a little too much to drink and I guess I was trying to be the big martyr. Maybe I just wasn't seeing things clearly or it would have been obvious you were just putting the moves on her."

"Putting the moves on her?" Reed replied, arching an eyebrow.

"Oh, excuse me," Andy said. "Maybe you city guys aren't familiar with that term. It's a phrase we commoners use out here in the sticks. It means using a girl to get your jollies."

Reed just stared at him. "I guess you feel you can talk to me like this because you're Jess's friend and you're doing it for her. But I have to tell you something, Andy. What I do with Jess is none of your goddamn business."

"You don't really give a crap about Jess, do you?" Andy said angrily. "To you she's just a toy to play with until you go back to your stupid prep school next month. God, you guys piss me off. People like you think you can take whatever you want."

Reed turned away.

"What do you think you're doing?" Andy shouted behind him.

Reed didn't answer. Suddenly he felt Andy grab his shoulder and try to stop him. Reed spun out of his grip and turned to face him.

"Back off, Moncure," Reed said forcefully.

"Listen," Andy said, stepping closer. "I'm dead serious, you jerk. And I think you'd better listen because I'm not drunk like I was the night of the party."

The next thing Reed knew, Andy raised his fists. Reed couldn't believe it. First the guy had the nerve to tell him what to do. Now he wanted to fight. Well, at this point it didn't matter whether they were lifeguards or not. Reed raised his fists. He'd be happy to oblige Andy.

"Hold it, you two," someone yelled.

Reed and Andy turned and saw Hank jogging toward them. "Am I seeing things, or were two of my best lifeguards about to have it out here in the parking lot?"

Reed shrugged. Andy stared down at an oil stain on the faded asphalt.

"Anyone want to tell me what this is about?"

Reed caught Andy's eye and stared at him silently.

"Yeah," Hank said with a nod. "I didn't think so." He turned to Andy. "It doesn't look like you're dressed to go to the beach, Andy. You're supposed to have the rest of the afternoon off, so why don't you try to find a place where you can cool off?"

Andy headed back to his car. Before he reached it, he turned around to see Hank and

Reed walking toward the lifeguard shack. Hank had put his hand on Reed's shoulder and they were talking about something. It didn't surprise Andy that Reed got preferential treatment once again. Everybody treated that guy like a prince.

FOUR

That evening the bus dropped Jess at the beach parking lot. She was wearing shorts and a white oxford shirt with the sleeves rolled up. She'd pulled her blonde hair back into a ponytail. Even though the beach officially closed at six P.M., the parking lot was still half-full, as if people were reluctant to leave the cool ocean waters and return inland where it promised to be an uncomfortably hot, sticky night.

The sun was dropping in the western sky. It was still yellow, but it would soon start to turn orange-red before disappearing below the horizon. Out in the water, in the absence of any significant wind, the waves curled gracefully before crashing rhythmically against the shore. Several fishing trawlers were headed back to Far Hampton harbor before dark. It had gone from a scorching hot day to a hot and sticky, yet beautiful evening.

Jess stopped at the edge of the beach and took off her tennis shoes, and then stepped onto the sand. Ahead she could see Reed in the Main chair, staring out at the water even though no one was swimming anymore. It was still warm and he wasn't wearing a shirt. As Jess walked toward him, she couldn't help staring at his muscular tanned back. The memories of touching those muscles returned to her. She could remember the smoothness of his skin and the hardness of his body, and she was suddenly filled with such strong yearning to feel them again that she had to stop and catch her breath.

Jess looked back at the parking lot. Maybe seeing Reed was a bad idea. Maybe she should turn around and go home. But then she looked up at him again and knew she couldn't leave. He was like a magnet drawing her to him. Reason and logic vanished as she got closer.

The important thing was to stay in control, she told herself. They were just going to talk. That was all. Nothing more. She stopped at the base of the chair.

"Working late?" she asked.

Reed looked down at her and smiled slightly. Jess felt everything start to stir inside her. She again reminded herself to stay in control.

"I guess," he replied. "Want to come up?"

"Okay." Jess climbed up the ladder and sat down on the opposite side of the bench from Reed. Almost out of habit, they both stared out at the water.

"Thanks for coming," Reed said.

"You don't have to thank me," Jess said.

"Well, I guess after all those phone calls you didn't return this week, I wasn't certain you'd actually show up tonight," Reed explained.

Jess turned and glanced at him. "I'm sorry about that, Reed. I just wasn't ready to talk to anyone."

"Except Andy," Reed said.

"That's true," Jess said. "But he's a friend."

Reed spun the strap of his lifeguard whistle around his finger. "And what am I?"

"It's different with you," Jess said. "You know that."

Their eyes met. Jess prayed Reed wouldn't press her on *how* it was different. Thankfully, Reed simply nodded. "You feel like you're ready to talk now?"

"Well, not exactly," Jess said. "But it's not right to keep avoiding you."

The last beach-goers were starting to pack up and leave now. Jess watched the sea gulls start to land for their evening meal of leftover food scraps.

"I guess the first thing I'd like to ask is why you feel you have to avoid me?" Reed asked.

"It's hard to explain," Jess said.

"Try?"

Jess took a deep breath and let it out slowly. "It just seems like when we're together everything goes wrong."

Reed was quiet for a moment. "You mean, because we were together on *Simplicity* and then the cops came and arrested me for the radar? And then we were together the night of the party and then Gary drowned?"

Jess nodded.

Reed bent forward and rested his elbows on his knees. He stared out at the ocean. "None of this has been easy for me, either, Jess. My brother betrayed me and Gary drowned. Both of those things could have happened even if we'd never met."

He straightened up and faced her. "In some way, knowing you has helped me, Jess. It's helped me to get through all this."

Jess stared back into his penetrating dark eyes. She'd been so busy thinking about her own pain that it hadn't occurred to her to think about his. But he had feelings, too. Jess felt her heart start to ache for him.

"I guess it's just hard for me to believe that

those things happened *because* we like each other," Reed said.

Jess could feel the ache in her heart grow as she remembered that rainy afternoon they'd shared in the cabin of his sailboat, and the night they'd held each other so passionately on the cool sand after the party. No, she couldn't think about that anymore.

"Jess?"

The sound of Reed's voice calling her name made her tremble. Oh, God, why had she agreed to meet him at the beach? She had to get out of there and never come back. She would call Hank later and tell him she was sorry, but she wouldn't be working as a lifeguard anymore.

"I'm sorry, Reed, but I think this is a bad idea," Jess said, reaching for the ladder. "I'd better go."

But before she could get out of the chair, Reed reached across and slid his hand around her arm. "Wait."

"No, Reed, I can't," Jess said, keeping her eyes averted so she didn't have to look at him.

"What are you afraid of, Jess?"

Jess just shook her head. She couldn't answer.

"This isn't right, Jess," Reed said. "I don't know what happened to make you change, but you at least owe me the courtesy of staying and talking."

"But it doesn't matter," Jess tried to say.

"It does to me," Reed said. "It matters — a lot."

Jess looked back at him and then sat back on the bench. Reed let go of her arm. "I'll stay for a while, Reed. But it would help if we didn't talk about us."

Reed leaned back in his corner and stared out at the waves. "I assume this has something to do with Andy. I mean, I saw the way he put his arm around your waist today at the funeral."

"Andy's my closest and dearest friend," Jess said. "He knows me better than anyone. If it weren't for him I don't know how I would have gotten through the last few days."

"How does he feel about you quitting the crew?" Reed asked.

Jess looked surprised. "How do you know about that?"

"He told me."

"When?"

"This afternoon," Reed said.

"Where?" Jess asked, puzzled.

"In the parking lot," Reed said. "I guess he made a special trip. To let me know."

"What else did he say?" Jess asked.

"He warned me not to lead you on," Reed said. "He seems to have this idea that I just want to use you. Then he decided he wanted to fight."

Jess stared at Reed in amazement. "Did you?"

"We would have, but Hank broke it up."

"Andy shouldn't have done that," she said.

"Are you serious about quitting?" Reed asked. Jess nodded.

"Is it because of me or Gary?"

"Both."

"Hank couldn't talk you out of it?"

"How do you know he even tried?" Jess asked.

"Because I know he thinks you're a good lifeguard," Reed said. "We all do. That's why it would hurt so much to see you quit for the wrong reasons."

"Letting Gary drown is the wrong reason?" Jess asked.

Reed nodded and leaned toward her, holding her with his intense gaze. "Listen, Jess, in the last two weeks I've experienced two really awful things. The first was when my brother set me up to be arrested. The second was when Gary drowned. You think I didn't want to beat the crap out of Billy when I found out what he'd done? I sure did. But instead I tried to learn from it. I learned that you can't ever turn your back.

Not even for a second. I think if I were to quit lifeguarding now it would be like saying that Gary's death was a total waste. I mean, I feel like I owe it to Gary to keep doing this so that it doesn't happen again."

Jess stared out at the ocean. Could Reed be right? The waves were becoming darker as the sun turned red-orange and began to sink toward the horizon. On the beach, two sea gulls were having a tug-of-war over a bag of potato chips. She felt a chill run up her arm as Reed slid his hand over hers.

"There's something else," Reed said. "I care about you, Jess. Maybe it's selfish, but I don't want you to quit. I want to know that when I come to this beach, you'll be here. It . . ." He paused and seemed to have trouble. "It gives me a reason to get out of bed in the morning."

Jess turned her hand over so that their palms met. She could feel the heat between their hands. It was the heat every part of her body felt when she touched him. If only she could touch him now. If only she could press her body against his. . . .

The sun was starting to disappear below the horizon. Jess knew it would be dark soon. Suddenly she knew she had to go. To be alone on the beach at night with Reed . . . it reminded her too much of what happened at the Sandy Dunes.

"Reed, I think I'd better go," she said, sliding her hand out of his.

"I can give you a ride."

"No, it's okay," Jess said quickly. "I'll take the beach bus." She reached for the ladder and started to climb down. Reed climbed down on the other side and started to walk alongside her back up the beach.

"For the second time today I promise I won't bite," Reed said.

"I know," Jess said.

"Besides, the beach bus only runs on the hour at this time of night and you just missed one," Reed said. "You'll have to wait an hour for the next one."

They reached the parking lot. Jess knew Reed was right. And yet the idea of getting into the jeep alone with him felt too close for comfort.

"I really don't mind waiting for the bus," Jess said. "I'll just — "

She didn't have time to finish the sentence. Reed suddenly took her arm and spun her around toward him. He held her there in the dark and they stared into each other's eyes. Their bodies pressed together; his skin warm against hers. Once again Jess felt the heat between them, and

remembered what it was like to be in his arms.
She felt her resolve melt as he pulled her close
and kissed her. She pressed her lips against his
and slid her hands around his taut, firm body.
If only she could stay in his arms forever. If only
there weren't all these other people and
complications. . . .

Paula Lewis's life had been hell since the Sandy
Dunes party. It had nothing to do with Gary
Pilot drowning. Instead it was because Reed had
clearly rejected her in favor of Little Miss Lifeguard Jess Sloat. Paula realized she'd taken Reed
for granted. Like a fool, she didn't realize what
she had until it was gone.

Not only that, but her plot to get Reed fired
from his stupid lifeguarding job had backfired.
Paula had tried to get him fired to keep him away
from Jess. Instead, Paula's relationship with Reed
was practically destroyed, and Billy now held a
terrible secret over her head. If he ever played
the tape he'd made in the church parking lot to
Reed, it would prove that she'd planted the dam-
aging letter and forged his name. That would
not only kill the relationship for good, but she'd
be in big trouble with the law.

Paula pulled her car up to the tall wrought-
iron gate at Breezes, the Petersens' estate. It was

dark and she was scared. The last thing she wanted to do was pay a visit to that creep Billy. But she had to get that tape from him. Paula reached out the window of her car and pressed the button on the intercom.

"Who is it?" Marvin, the butler, asked through the speaker.

"Paula. Is Billy there?" She knew he was. He had a curfew.

"Just one minute please."

Paula waited. A moment later a new voice crackled over the intercom.

"What do you want, Paula?" It was Billy.

"I have to see you," Paula insisted.

"Oh, yeah?" Billy sounded amused.

"Please, Billy," Paula begged.

"Give me one good reason."

"It will be worth your while," Paula promised. "I swear."

The next thing she knew, the black gates began to swing open. Paula drove in and parked in the circular driveway. Marvin opened the front door.

"Billy will see you in his room, Miss Lewis," he said.

Paula went up the stairs. She knew Billy's room was down the hall from Reed's. The door was open and loud music was coming from inside. Paula stepped in. The room was an absolute wreck. Clothes, videotapes, and CDs were strewn all over the place. The bed was unmade and covered with clothes. An amazing amount of electronic equipment was lying around, including video cameras, VCRs, TV monitors, and lots of black cables connecting them.

Across the room, Billy sat with his back to Paula at a table cluttered with electronic junk.

"Billy?" Paula said nervously, still standing in the doorway.

"Come in and close the door," Billy said without turning around.

Paula stepped in and closed the door behind her. Billy still hadn't turned to look at her. He seemed to be working on something.

"Aren't you going to ask me why I'm here?" Paula asked.

"I know why you're here," Billy said, his back still turned.

Paula looked around uncomfortably. She didn't understand why he wouldn't turn around and face her. Suddenly out of the corner of her eye, she noticed something lying on a shelf near her. It was the tape recorder Billy had used that afternoon! Paula quickly glanced back at Billy.

He seemed totally involved with whatever it was he was doing. She quickly reached for the tape recorder and slid it into her pocket.

"Great!" Billy shouted and turned around. He had a big smile on his face. "You were perfect, Paula."

"What are you talking about?" Paula asked nervously.

"I've got it all on tape," Billy said. He stood up and pointed to a small black video camera mounted on a shelf above him. Billy climbed up on a stool and took the camera down.

"See the lens?" he asked, pointing at the camera's lens as he walked toward Paula. "It's wide angle so it gets almost half the room. I was watching everything you did on that monitor and recording it on videotape."

Billy pointed back at the table he'd been sitting at and Paula saw a small black-and-white TV. Next to it a VCR was running. As Paula watched the screen she saw herself enter the room, close the door, and then take the tape recorder off the shelf. Meanwhile Billy held his hand out toward her.

"The tape I made of you this afternoon isn't in it," he said. "But I'd still like the tape recorder back."

Feeling her face turn red, Paula reached into

her pocket and handed him the recorder. Billy grinned and put it back on the shelf.

"Thanks, Paula," Billy said. "You've been a great help."

"Okay, Billy," Paula said, feeling totally humiliated. "You've had your fun. Now I have to talk to you."

"Sure, Paula," Billy said cheerfully. "What can I do for you?"

Paula looked around. "I don't want to talk here."

"Afraid I might tape you again?" Billy asked.

Paula nodded.

"Okay, let's go outside." Billy led her out of the room and down the hall to a set of French doors. They went out onto a balcony overlooking the ocean. The air felt cooler this close to the water and the waves crashed in the moonlight. Billy took a cigarette out of his pocket and lit it. He started to put the pack away, then pulled it back out and offered it to Paula.

"Oops, how vulgar of me," he said. "Want one?"

"No, thanks," Paula replied. She hugged herself and stared out at the dark ocean. "How do I know you're not recording me right now?"

"I'm not," Billy said.

"Why should I believe you?" Paula asked.

"Frisk me if you like." Billy held out his arms and spread his legs. Paula stared at him in disbelief. The thought of sliding her hands around him disgusted her.

"I guess I'll just take your word," Paula said with a shrug. She opened her bag and took out five new $100 bills. "I'll give you five hundred dollars for that tape."

"I'm impressed," Billy said.

"Then take it," Paula urged him.

"I guess that tape means a lot to you," Billy said.

"Yes, it does," she said. "Now please take the money."

But Billy just smiled and shook his head. Paula clenched her fists. God, how he infuriated her!

"If you don't want money, then tell me what you do want," Paula said.

"What are you willing to give me?" Billy asked.

Paula took a deep breath and swallowed. "Whatever you want, Billy."

"You sure?"

"Yes." Paula nodded and grit her teeth.

Billy stepped toward her. Paula shut her eyes. She couldn't believe what she was about to do, but she had no choice. A moment passed. Suddenly Paula realized Billy hadn't touched her. She opened her eyes and saw that he'd walked past her to the French doors.

"Come on, Paula," he said.

"Why?" Paula asked, confused.

"Just come inside," Billy said.

Paula stepped back into the house and looked around nervously. "Where are we going?"

"You're going home," Billy said.

"But I thought you wanted something from me," Paula said.

"I do," Billy said. "But not quite yet."

The next thing Paula knew, Billy went back down the hall and into his room. He closed the door, leaving Paula to find her way out alone. It was typical of Billy to be so rude. She went downstairs and started to cross the foyer toward the door. Marvin wasn't around, so she assumed she'd let herself out. She was just reaching for the door when the knob started to turn. Paula stepped back and the door swung open.

She was face to face with Reed.

For a moment he just stood there and stared at her with a smile on his face. Paula wondered if it were possible that he was happy to see her. Then the smile changed into a slight smirk and Reed stepped in and closed the door behind him.

"You looked so happy a second ago," Paula said. "For a moment I thought maybe you were happy to see me."

"To what do I owe the pleasure of this visit?" Reed asked in a mocking tone.

"I was here to see Billy," Paula said.

"Oh? What about?"

"It was personal."

"Personal between you and Billy?" Reed gave her a curious look. "Now *that's* interesting."

Paula had to get off that subject fast. Besides, there was something she'd been wanting to say to Reed. "I know you probably hate me."

Reed slid his hands into his pockets and pursed his lips. "Hate you? No, Paula, I don't hate you. I might be really disappointed in you, but I don't hate you."

"Reed, whatever I did . . . whatever I said . . . I did it because I really care for you. Maybe I was stupid and self-centered, but it was because I couldn't stand the thought of losing you to that girl."

"Jess?"

Paula stared at the marble floor and nodded. She was terrified that Reed would laugh at her. But he didn't. Instead he said, "I'm sorry it didn't work out between us."

Paula looked up and studied Reed's handsome face. Suddenly she knew she shouldn't have worried about him laughing at her. Reed was too good to do that. Realizing how good he was only made Paula miss him more. He seemed truly sincere when he said he was sorry it hadn't worked out. Suddenly Paula knew she was going to cry. She quickly stretched up on her toes and kissed him on the lips, then turned and pulled the door open and ran out into the dark.

"Paula?" Reed called behind her from the doorway. "Are you okay?"

"Yes, Reed," Paula called back. But she didn't turn around. She didn't want him to see the tears falling down her cheeks.

Jess was sitting in her kitchen when someone knocked on the front door. She looked up apprehensively; she wasn't expecting anyone. She got up and went to the door, but didn't open it. "Who is it?"

"So? How'd it go?" a voice asked.

Jess felt a moment of relief. It was Andy. But her relief quickly turned into agitation. She pulled open the door.

"I think we'd better talk," she said as Andy stepped in.

"Uh-oh, you're pissed about something," Andy said. "Reed tell you about our little run-in at the beach this afternoon?"

"Yes."

"Jess?" her father yelled from the den.

"Yes, Dad?"

"Someone here?"

"It's just Andy."

"Okay. I forgot to tell you Hank Diamond called before. He said he had to go somewhere tonight and you could call him first thing in the morning."

"Thanks, Dad." Jess led Andy through the house and out to the screened-in porch in the back. Usually the air cooled at night, but tonight it was almost as bad as it had been during the day. Andy sat down on one of the lounges, but Jess remained standing with her arms crossed.

"I appreciate your concern for me, Andy, but I'm really capable of dealing with Reed Petersen myself," she said.

"So what happened?" Andy asked.

The memory of Reed kissing her flashed through her head. "Nothing happened. We talked."

"About what?"

Suddenly Jess resented the way Andy was

prying into her personal business. Why did it bother her now? she wondered. For the past few days there hadn't been anything they couldn't discuss with each other.

"Mostly about whether or not I was going to continue as a lifeguard," Jess said. That was the truth, but it felt a little strange to Jess that she wasn't telling him the whole truth.

"I didn't realize Reed cared so much about whether or not you're a lifeguard," Andy said.

"Well, I think I've decided that I'm going to stay with it," Jess said.

Andy just nodded. "So he changed your mind."

Jess didn't like his tone of voice. It sounded accusatory. "No, Andy, Reed didn't change my mind," she said. "I did. He just helped me see the whole thing from a different perspective."

"What perspective was that?" Andy asked.

"What a waste it would be if I quit now," Jess explained. "If I keep at it, it's like I'm keeping Gary's memory alive. Like maybe I can use what I've learned so that it won't happen again."

"That's very admirable of you," Andy said.

"Do you really mean that?" Jess asked uncertainly.

"Yes," Andy said. "What else did you two talk about?"

"Just everything that's happened," Jess replied.

"And what did you decide?"

Again Andy's interrogation bothered her. But Jess knew she couldn't say anything about it. After all, he was her best friend.

"We didn't decide anything, Andy," Jess said. "We just talked."

"One last question," Andy said. "Where did you leave it?"

"I don't know what you mean," Jess said.

"I mean, where did you leave it between you two?" Andy asked. "Are you going to start seeing him again?"

"At the beach," Jess said innocently. "I mean, if we're both lifeguards . . ."

"That's not what I meant," Andy said, getting up and stepping close to her. "I meant, are you two going to start seeing each other the way you were seeing each other before Gary drowned?"

Jess shook her head. "I have no plans to do that, Andy."

"Good." The next thing Jess knew, Andy put his arms around her and hugged her. She stood motionless in his arms and made no attempt to hug him back. After a moment he pulled back slightly and pressed his forehead against hers.

"I know it must not be easy, Jess," he said. "But that guy's just not good for you. I wouldn't be saying this if it wasn't true."

"I know," Jess said.

FIVE

The next morning Jess called Hank and told him she'd be reporting to work that day. Hank was glad and didn't seem to mind when Jess asked if he would switch her chair assignment. Up to the night Gary drowned, Jess had sat with Reed. When Hank asked why she wanted to change, Jess simply said it was personal.

She was waiting at the bus stop when Lisa's yellow VW bug pulled up.

"I see you got this thing to work," Jess said.

"I didn't," Lisa said with a smile. "My father did. I just paid for the parts. So you wouldn't be standing here waiting for the bus because you're going to work, would you?"

"Matter of fact, I am," Jess replied.

"All right!" Lisa pushed open the passenger door. "Hop in."

Jess got in and they headed for the beach. As Lisa accelerated, the VW bug roared loudly.

"I thought you said your father fixed this car," Jess said.

"He fixed the brakes," Lisa said. "Now I have to save up for a new muffler."

"Good luck," Jess said.

"I was really scared you were going to quit," Lisa said as she drove. "I mean, we're the two rookie girls. We gotta stick together." She held up her hand for a high five and Jess slapped it.

"So what changed your mind?" Lisa asked.

"Nothing really changed it," Jess said. "I mean, I never actually decided to quit. I was just thinking about quitting, that's all. Then I had a talk with Reed and he got me to look at it in a different way and I decided to stay."

Lisa gave her a quick wide-eyed glance. "That's right! Last night was your big talk with Reed. How did it go?"

"It wasn't very big," Jess said. "We mostly talked about Gary and why I should still be a lifeguard."

"That's all?"

"Pretty much," Jess said.

"So are you guys going to go back to sharing the Main chair?"

Jess shook her head. "I asked Hank to switch me to another chair. He said he would. I think he was just glad to have me back on the crew."

"So who are you going to sit with?" Lisa asked.

"I don't know. I guess I'll find out when I get there."

They reached the beach road and turned toward the Far Hampton public beach. It was another hot day. All the courts at the Beach and Tennis Club were empty. In the distance someone was flying a kite with a long dragonlike tail.

"Can I ask one more nosy question?" Lisa asked.

"Why not?" Jess replied.

"How are things between you and Andy?"

"Okay, I guess," Jess responded with a shrug.

"It seems like you two have gotten a lot closer since everything happened," Lisa said.

"Andy and I were always close," Jess replied. "We just drifted apart a little when the summer began. But now it's back to normal."

"More like the way it's always been?" Lisa asked. "I mean, like really good friends, but nothing more?"

Jess glanced at her and smiled. "I guess you could say that."

"So, did you hear about the party?" Lisa asked.

"No, what party?"

"Hank asked me and Reed to have a party for the crew," Lisa said. "Everyone's been so bummed out since Gary died. I guess he hopes this will revive their spirits."

Jess nodded. She wasn't certain she was up to a party right now.

"Reed said we could use his father's cabin cruiser," Lisa said.

Jess was surprised. "I didn't know his father had a cabin cruiser."

"Reed said he has it for business reasons, except it hardly ever gets used," Lisa said. "It was named after his mother and after she died his father couldn't deal with it. So it just sits in the harbor most of the time."

"Well, I guess it's pretty nice of him to let us use it," Jess said.

"So, do you think you'll come?" Lisa asked.

"Me?" Jess asked, surprised.

"Yeah, Jess, you," Lisa said. "You're a lifeguard, remember?"

"When are you going to have it?" Jess asked.

Lisa had to think about that. "Well, Andy said he was going to his cousins' for a week. So I guess we better do it after that."

"And this is sidewalk sales week," Jess said.

"You're right!" Lisa gasped. "We couldn't let

the party interfere with the one week of the year I might be able to afford to buy something around here."

"Right," Jess agreed.

A few minutes later they arrived at the beach and parked behind the lifeguard shack. Hank's van was already there so they knew he was probably inside the shack. Ellie Sax was just getting off her bicycle, and when she saw Jess, she came over.

"You're back?" Ellie asked.

Jess nodded.

"I'm glad." Ellie gave her a hug.

Soon Stu and Andy arrived, and then Jess saw Reed's jeep pull into the lot and head toward them. When everyone was assembled, Hank came out of the lifeguard shack.

"I've got new chair assignments," he announced. "Malibu and Dunes chairs remain the same. Ellie and Jess will be in the West Wing. Stu and Andy will be in the East Wing. Now get to your stations. It's supposed to be in the nineties again today, so we're going to be busy."

As the news of the seating changes sank in, the guards responded in different ways. Jess was actually relieved that she would be sitting with Ellie and not one of the guys. She couldn't quite explain why. It just seemed to take a certain pressure off her. She turned and looked at Andy. He was smiling, but she wondered if he wasn't secretly disappointed. She had a feeling he'd hoped he'd get to sit with her.

It took Lisa a moment to realize who her senior guard was. As usual, Hank hadn't bothered to announce the final seating or chair. To him it was a logical process of deduction. To Lisa it meant she'd be sitting with Reed in the Main chair.

The guards headed for their chairs. The beach hadn't officially opened yet, but people were already in the waves, swimming at their own risk.

Lisa climbed up into the Main chair and slid into the corner of the bench seat. She'd never sat in that chair before, and she could see why it was the toughest chair on the beach. While there were hardly any patroons — as Andy called them — sitting in front of the wing chairs, there was already a small crowd in front of hers. Reed climbed up next to her and quietly nodded as if to welcome her to the chair. Then he sat down and began the relentless task of watching over the patrons.

It took an hour before Lisa could even bring herself to say anything to him. Of course it wasn't as if they were strangers or anything. She'd ridden in Reed's jeep and talked to him several times. But never alone. This was something new. So she'd waited that first hour to see if he'd say anything to her, but he didn't. Lisa knew Reed took his job very seriously. For the past hour he'd sat almost stock still in the chair. The only thing that moved were his eyes as he scanned the beach and water for potential problems.

"I, uh, think it's really great that you talked Jess into coming back to work," Lisa finally said.

"I didn't really talk her into it," Reed replied without turning to look at her. "I just asked her to look at quitting in a different way."

"Well, whatever you did, it worked," Lisa said.

She watched Reed nod. Then he stood up and blew his whistle at some guys throwing a football around in the water. Cupping his hands together he shouted, "No ball playing in the water!"

The guys stopped playing and Reed sat down again.

"Oh, Reed," Lisa said. "I talked to Jess about the party. We agreed that we should wait until Andy gets back from his trip."

Reed sat up a little straighter. "He's going somewhere?"

"To his cousins' in New Hampshire, I think," Lisa said.

"Good," Reed said.

The afternoon was brutally hot. Even under their chair umbrellas the lifeguards were suffering. Reed tried to watch the patrons, but he kept getting distracted. He knew what was bothering him.

"Can I ask you a question?" he said, without looking at Lisa.

"Uh, sure," Lisa replied, caught by surprise.

"Did Jess have something to do with Hank changing the seating assignments?"

Lisa nodded. "She asked him to."

"Thanks." Reed glanced down the beach and saw Jess climb down from the West Wing chair.

"I'm going to get something to drink," he said. "Want anything?"

"Why don't I go?" Lisa said quickly. Reed suspected that the thought of being left alone on the busiest chair on the beach on such a crowded day scared her.

"No, I can get it for myself," he said. "I think it's important that you see what it's like to sit alone. And don't worry, I'm only going up to the snack bar. If there's a problem, just give me two short blasts on the whistle and I'll be right there."

"You sure you want to leave me?" Lisa asked uncertainly.

"Don't worry," Reed assured her. "You'll do fine."

Reed climbed down the ladder. He'd meant what he'd said to Lisa about the experience of being in the chair alone. But he also had to admit that part of the reason he wanted to go to the snack bar was in the hope that Jess was headed there, too. The sand was scorching and all around him people were skipping quickly across it as if they were dancing on hot coals. Reed knew a trick for walking on hot sand. It meant walking slowly, but if you slid your feet under the top layer of sand, it was cooler underneath.

Not far away, Jess was walking quickly toward the snack bar, almost hopping from spot to spot to save her burning feet. She was so preoccupied with getting across the scorching sand that she didn't even see Reed until she was only a few yards away from him. Suddenly she looked up and stopped, caught off guard.

"Sand's pretty hot," Reed said.

An embarrassed smile crossed Jess's lips. "I must look pretty silly hopping around like this."

"It's hard to imagine you looking silly, Jess," Reed said, gazing intensely at her. "To me you always look beautiful, even when you're hopping."

Jess's eyes seemed to glaze over for a moment and Reed wondered if she was thinking back to the evening before when they'd kissed. Then Jess shook her head as if she were trying to snap out of it.

"Headed for the snack bar?" Reed asked.

"Uh, no," Jess replied.

Reed frowned. Jess had several dollar bills clenched in her hand. He looked up and their eyes met.

"Oh, uh, what am I saying?" Jess quickly corrected herself. "Yes, that's where I'm going."

"Sun's so hot it's hard to think straight," Reed said, as if to make an excuse for her.

Jess nodded and together they started walking toward the snack bar. Once again Reed felt that peculiar sensation he only seemed to feel around Jess. She made him feel more alive and aware than normal. Being with her was like breathing pure oxygen.

"So how do you like sitting with Ellie?" he asked.

"I like it," Jess nodded vigorously. "It's such

a relief to be sitting with another — " The words had started to come out before Jess even realized what she was about to say.

"With another what?" Reed asked, puzzled.

"Uh, nothing," Jess said quickly.

"I don't get it," Reed said.

"It doesn't matter," Jess said. "Believe me, it's not important."

But Reed wouldn't let it go. "Another . . . lifeguard? No, you've always sat with lifeguards. Another . . . girl?"

Jess nodded. She felt herself blush. Thank God she had a good tan. They got to the snack bar line.

"Why is it a relief to sit with another girl?" Reed asked.

Jess looked straight into his eyes as if she were leveling with him. "You know why."

Reed smiled. "I didn't realize sitting with guys was such a problem."

"It isn't a problem," Jess said. "But it sometimes creates a problem."

"Like us, Jess?" Reed asked. "Were we a problem?"

Jess stared down at the sand. She knew that he was saying he still liked her and didn't understand why they had to break up. "Not us. It just seems like when we're together there are too many other problems. Too much pain."

The snack line inched forward, but Jess and Reed were almost oblivious to the others in line around them.

"I thought we worked that out," Reed said. "In the parking lot . . ."

Jess couldn't look him in the eye. Yes, for that one moment when she'd been in his arms, everything felt better. But when she wasn't in his arms, it began to feel bad and uncertain again.

"I still feel like it could happen all over again," Jess said. "Only God knows what might happen next."

"Maybe nothing might happen," Reed said.

But Jess shook her head and looked away. It was too risky and the stakes were too great. *Gary was dead.* . . .

She felt Reed's hand go around her arm and gently turn her toward him.

"Listen to me," he said softly, leaning close.

Jess felt almost helpless. She could feel that magnetic sensation drawing her to him. At close range it was almost overpowering.

"Yes, Reed?" she whispered. She sensed that he was going to say something serious. She wondered if he would make her change her mind about him. She felt as if part of her was already wishing he would.

"Hey, guys, I hope I'm not interrupting anything."

Jess and Reed turned around. Andy was standing behind them panting. Beads of sweat on his forehead were collecting and running down his temples and nose. He must have run a long distance, maybe all the way from the East Wing chair.

"Uh, no." Jess said as Reed let go of her arm and she backed away. "Of course not."

"Oh, good," Andy said. "How's it going, Reed?"

"Okay, Andy," Reed replied. "Pretty hot day to be running."

"Uh, yeah," Andy said.

"Guess you ran because the sand is so hot," Reed said.

Andy nodded. Jess had a feeling he'd run because he'd seen something in the snack bar line that he didn't like — her and Reed together.

Andy wiped the sweat off his brow with his hand. "You guys getting drinks?"

Reed and Jess nodded. Andy turned again toward Reed.

"Isn't it usually a junior guard's job to get drinks?" Andy asked. "I mean, if anyone stays in the chair alone, shouldn't it be the senior guard?"

"I think it's a good experience for a rookie," Reed said.

"Oh, sure, I agree," Andy said. "On a day when it's not too crowded. But on a day like today don't you think it's a little risky?"

"If I did I wouldn't be standing here, would I?" Reed asked.

"I don't know," Andy said, glancing from Reed to Jess. "I guess it depends how thirsty you are."

Reed couldn't help but smile. "I guess I'm pretty thirsty."

"I get the feeling we all are," Andy said.

The line moved ahead and it was almost time for the lifeguards to get drinks. Jess kept her eyes fixed on the snack counter and on the kids inside hastily serving drinks and food. Even without looking at Reed or talking to him, Jess could still feel his presence. She found herself wishing Andy wasn't there, but she quickly forced the thought away.

Andy wasn't the only person on the beach who'd noticed that Jess was standing in the snack bar line talking with Reed. Crouching behind the dunes, having a cigarette, Billy had also seen it. As punishment for stealing the radar, it was now Billy's community service job to spend each day dragging a large black garbage bag along the beach, spearing litter on a stick with a long metal point on its end.

It was a miserable, hot job and Billy hated it. He hated wearing the town park's stupid summer khaki uniform of high socks, baggy shorts, a short-sleeved shirt, and pith helmet. He hated crisscrossing the beach day after day, picking up litter and putting it in the bag.

Most of all, he hated being noticed. He wore dark sunglasses and tried to be as inconspicuous as possible, but every once in a while he caught someone staring and smiling as if they remembered when the garbage collector had been a big shot senior lifeguard.

Billy took another drag off his cigarette and laughed at Andy Moncure racing across the hot sand to join Reed and Jess. It was pretty obvious, wasn't it? Reed and Jess were getting back together again and Andy was jealous. But not as jealous as Billy. He was a garbage collector with a nine P.M. curfew while Reed sat in the Main chair soaking in adoration and staying out as late as he wanted. Once again Reed had come out on top and Billy was on the bottom.

Billy watched the adoring way Jess looked at his brother. God, it made him sick. He could still remember how happy he'd been when Paula promised him that she'd get him Jess. To Billy it had sounded like the perfect revenge against his brother and he'd been naive enough to think that Paula could really do it. He'd been too dumb to realize that Paula was just using him to get what *she* wanted, namely Reed.

But Billy had never forgotten the perfect revenge. And now that it looked as if his brother was getting back together with Jess Sloat, he had an idea of how to do it. Especially since he could now get Paula to do anything he wanted.

At the end of the day the lifeguards slowly trudged back up to the lifeguard shack. It had been a long, hot day, and the beach had gotten so crowded that it had been hard to tell where the sand ended and the water began. The guards had seen a lot of bad sunburns, several cases of dehydration, and at least one sunstroke victim who had to be taken by ambulance to the Far Hampton medical center.

Lisa and Jess sat in the shade at the edge of the porch, sipping cups of watery lemonade drawn from a big plastic cooler Hank had put out. Jess rubbed her fingers against her forehead. It felt as if her skin was caked with a layer of coarse powder.

"It's salt," Stu said as he sat on the porch with his back against the wall. "You know it's hot when the sweat dries on your forehead and leaves salt."

"It was like a sauna today," said Lisa.

Reed stepped onto the porch and poured himself some lemonade. Jess noticed that he kept glancing at her when the others weren't looking. She knew he wanted to speak to her. He hadn't had a chance to say much on the snack bar line before Andy had joined them. Now Andy was down at the Malibu chair doing something for Hank. Reed walked right up to her, even though Jess was still with Lisa.

"Uh, Jess?" he said.

"Yes, Reed?"

"Think I could talk to you alone?"

"I'd rather not, Reed," Jess said.

Reed glanced at Lisa and back to Jess. "Would you like a ride home?"

Jess turned to Lisa. "Uh, thanks, but Lisa will give me a ride. It's on her way."

Reed pressed his lips together and nodded. Jess could see how frustrated he was that she was avoiding him. She couldn't really blame him. If only she wasn't so unsure. If only she knew what to do.

Finally Reed gave up and walked away toward his jeep.

"Maybe you should have talked to him," Lisa said.

Jess just sighed and shook her head. "God, I wish I knew what to do."

"Well, we might as well go home," Lisa said. "I've had enough of this beach for one day."

They got up and headed for Lisa's car. Halfway across the parking lot they heard someone shout, "Wait, Jess!"

Jess turned and saw Andy jogging toward them.

"You think I could talk to you alone?" Andy panted as he caught up to them.

Lisa gave Jess a funny look. "I think I hear an echo."

Andy scowled at her and then looked across the parking lot where Reed was getting into his jeep. Then he sort of grimaced and nodded as if he now understood what Lisa had meant.

"What do you want to talk about, Andy?" Jess asked.

"Just come with me and I'll tell you," Andy said.

Jess looked uncertainly at Lisa. She really

didn't want to talk to Andy, either. Everything was getting so complicated and she felt as if she were in the middle of it all.

"Jess?" Andy said. "You coming?"

It had been easier to say no to Reed. But Andy was another story. He'd been so supportive. She owed it to him.

"Okay, Andy."

"I'll just take her for a moment," Andy said to Lisa.

Lisa nodded silently. As Jess walked away with Andy she could see her friend wasn't happy.

They walked along the sandy edge of the parking lot, avoiding the scattered brown and green glass from broken beer bottles and globs of melted gum. Andy shoved his hands into the pockets of his orange bathing suit.

"Look, Jess, I know I shouldn't say this, but I'm worried about you," he said. "I mean, about you and Reed."

Jess just nodded. That was no surprise.

"I mean, you've been back on the job one day and already it's obvious what's happening," Andy said.

"It is?" Jess asked, not exactly sure what he meant.

"Aw, give me a break, Jess," Andy said, exasperated. "He's coming on to you. He wants to get back together."

"It's not up to him," Jess said simply.

"Oh, come on, Jess."

Suddenly Jess stopped and stared at him. Was Andy saying that she had no ability to control her own life? "What do you think he's going to do, Andy? Kidnap me?"

"No," Andy replied. "He's going to do the same stuff he did before. He's going to wow you with his car and his boat and his mansion and his preppy friends and his money. He's going to make you think you could be one of them. He's going to suck you in and use you and then dump you when he feels like it."

"That's *not* what he did," Jess said.

"That's what he would have done," Andy insisted. "If fate hadn't interfered."

"I still don't see why he'd want to do that," Jess replied. "But even if he did, what makes you think I'd just go along with it, Andy? I mean, what do you think I am, a bimbo?"

"No!" Andy said. "I don't think you're a bimbo. I think you're really smart. It's just that . . . well, I mean . . ."

"What, Andy?"

Andy shook his head. "Okay, you want to

know what I really think? I think you're really smart and really great, but like everyone else you've got weaknesses. And your weakness is rich, good-looking guys."

Jess put her hands on her hips and rolled her eyes. "Oh, sure, Andy. Like I've had so much experience with them."

"Maybe you haven't," Andy said. "But I saw what happened when you started seeing Reed. It was like you totally forgot who you were and where you came from and who your friends were."

"Is that true, Andy?" Jess asked. "Or is it just that I didn't pay as much attention to *you*?"

Jess expected Andy to get angry, but he didn't. Instead he just stood there and stared at her for a moment without saying anything.

"Well?" Jess asked.

"Well, look at us, Jess," Andy said calmly. "Here we are, two people who are supposed to be such good friends. I mean, ever since Gary drowned we've been closer than ever, right? We've depended so much on each other. Now what in the world would make us fight like this? Don't you see, Jess? It's Reed. He comes back into your life and everything instantly gets turned upside down."

Jess had been all ready for a fight, but now

she felt the anger drain out of her. Was Andy right? The days since Gary drowned had been horrible, but she'd never felt closer to her friends. Now Reed was returning to her life and suddenly all these problems were cropping up again.

She sighed and slid her hands around Andy's waist to give him a hug. "All right, Andy, I get the point."

"You know, tomorrow morning I'm supposed to leave to visit my cousins for a week," Andy said. "I almost feel like canceling the trip."

"Don't, Andy. I swear I'll be okay. Really."

"So what are you going to do?" Andy asked.

Jess backed away, a little surprised. "Do about what?"

"About Reed."

"I don't know," Jess said with a shrug. She slid her hand into Andy's and started to pull him back toward Lisa. "But I'm not ignoring what you said, Andy. Believe me."

Lisa had watched Jess and Andy walk away. She'd seen them start to talk and then watched as the discussion seemed to turn into an argument. Then she saw them hug and make up. Lisa liked Jess a lot. But what she was doing to Andy wasn't fair. Lisa knew they were very close friends, but it almost seemed as if Jess was leading Andy on. Now she watched as Jess and Andy returned from their talk, walking hand in hand.

"Everything straightened out?" she asked.

"For now," Andy replied.

For an awkward moment the three of them stood in the parking lot. Then Andy nodded back toward his mother's car. "Guess I'd better get going. I've got to pack for my trip."

"I hope you have a good time," Lisa said.

Andy nodded, but it was almost as if he didn't hear her. He was staring straight at Jess.

"You sure you'll be all right?" he asked.

Jess nodded.

"All right. I'll call you from New Hampshire." Andy stepped close and kissed her on the forehead, then started away.

"Have a good trip!" Jess waved. Then she and Lisa started walking toward Lisa's VW bug again.

"Everything okay?" Lisa asked as they got in and she started to drive out of the parking lot.

"Who knows?" Jess replied with a shrug and stared out the window.

Lisa was really curious to find out what was going on between Jess and Andy, but she could see Jess wasn't in the mood to talk about it. Suddenly she had an idea.

"Hey, what do you say we hit the sidewalk sale?"

Jess looked uncertain. "You think?"

"Sure," Lisa said. "You know what they say. When the going gets tough, the tough go shopping."

It was the first night of sidewalk sales week in Far Hampton. Every summer for one week, the merchants were allowed to display all their sale items on the sidewalks. For that week the town always felt a little like an outdoor market with people strolling along, bargaining with merchants for the things they had on sale.

Soon Lisa and Jess were making their way past the tables of odd-sized basketball sneakers and slightly damaged children's toys. They stopped at Jeanius, their favorite too-expensive clothes store.

"It looked for a moment like you and Andy had a little fight," Lisa said as they sorted through the racks of jeans and blouses marked on sale.

Jess nodded. "It's so hard. I know he cares about me and doesn't want to see me get hurt. I just wish I knew what to do."

"About Andy or about Reed?" Lisa asked.

"Both," Jess replied.

"Well, do you really like Andy?" Lisa asked.

"Absolutely," Jess said.

"As a very good friend, or as more?" Lisa asked.

"I don't know."

"Oh, come on, Jess, of course you do," Lisa said.

Jess knew Lisa was right. But it wasn't that simple. She held up a purple blouse made of thin billowy material. "What do you think?"

"I think it's a little too see-through," Lisa said.

"You're right." Jess sighed and put it back on the rack. "The thing I hate is that it feels like I have to make a choice. Like it's either Andy or Reed. And I don't want to make that choice. I *can't* make that choice."

"Does Reed say you have to make that choice?" Lisa asked.

"No, it's Andy mostly," Jess admitted

Lisa pulled a pair of jeans off the rack. They had rows of silver studs running along the seams. "Am I crazy?"

"Totally," Jess said.

Lisa put the jeans back. "It doesn't seem right. I mean, if Andy is your friend and he really wants what's best for you, why should he stop you from seeing Reed?"

Jess shrugged. "I guess deep down inside

Andy would like us to be more than just good friends."

"But you said you don't feel that way," Lisa said.

"I don't," Jess said, but then she quickly caught herself. "Oh, I don't know. Sometimes I wish I did. It would be so easy then. I mean, I do feel like Andy and I fit so well together."

"So you're sort of leading him on until you make up your mind?" Lisa asked.

"No!" Jess gasped. "I mean, that's not what I want to do. I'd never do that."

"Jess . . ." Lisa gave her a knowing look.

"It's hard, Lisa," Jess said matter-of-factly. "Maybe I'm not sure how I feel about Andy, but the one thing I do know is that I don't want to hurt him."

"Oh, so you're leading him on because you don't want to hurt him," Lisa said.

"No!" Jess insisted. Then she sighed. "Oh, I don't know." She gazed over at Lisa. "You like Andy, don't you?"

Lisa nodded.

"Do you want me to say something to him?" Jess asked.

"No!" Lisa stared at her in disbelief. "Are you serious? That would be death."

"Why?" Jess asked.

"Because there's only one person in his life right now and that's you," Lisa said.

"I think you're right," Jess said. "Oh, God, Lisa, I'm really sorry. Now I feel like I'm keeping Andy from you. I really don't mean to do that. It's just that I don't know what I'd do without him right now."

The girls left Jeanius. Even on sale, the items inside were too expensive.

"Hungry?" Lisa asked.

Jess shook her head. "It's too hot."

"Want to go sit in Rafe's?" Lisa said. "It's air conditioned."

"Why don't we just sit on a bench?" Jess suggested.

"Okay."

They found a bench on the sidewalk where they could sit and watch the shoppers pass. Lisa was quiet for a long time.

"I hope you're not mad at me," Jess finally said.

"I feel like I should be," Lisa admitted. "But I'm not. Maybe it's because I know what you've been through. It's just that it seemed like things were going so well with you and Reed up to the point where Gary drowned. I don't understand why you won't see him now."

"It's complicated," Jess said. "It's partly because I'm afraid I'll lose Andy as a friend. It's partly because when Reed and I get together everything just seems to go wrong. And it's partly because maybe I think Andy's right — school's going to start in a month and Reed's going to go away."

"Haven't you ever heard of a long-distance relationship?" Lisa asked.

"Yes," Jess said. "But that doesn't mean I want to get into one. . . . Especially with Reed."

"Why especially with Reed?" Lisa asked.

"I don't know," Jess shrugged. "I just . . . maybe I'm listening too much to Andy about all of Reed's sophisticated city friends and the parties and vacations and everything. Andy just makes it sound like there's so much going on in Reed's life that if I wasn't physically there he'd forget about me."

"Do you think it's true?" Lisa asked.

"Who knows?" Jess said. "I mean, it doesn't seem true from what I've seen this summer. All Reed seems to do is work as a lifeguard and then go home at night and work on his sailboat. He says he'd like to spend the winter preparing to sail across the Atlantic Ocean next summer."

"By himself?" Lisa asked.

"I'm not really sure," Jess said. "We only

talked about it once and he didn't say if he wanted to go with anyone else."

"Well, it sure doesn't sound like he plans to spend the winter partying," Lisa said.

Jess nodded and watched the people pass on the sidewalk. Maybe Lisa was right.

SIX

Billy stood by the window of his room and watched as Reed walked down to the dock to work on his sailboat, *Simplicity*. On most nights, Reed would stay on the dock until dark and sometimes even later.

There were still a few hours before Billy's curfew and he told Marvin he was going out for a walk on the beach. Billy went out the back door, around the pool, and headed down to the beach. But as soon as he was out of sight of the house, he doubled back through the dunes, and cut through a corner of the yard to the garage. There he quietly opened the garage door and got into his jeep and left.

Billy drove into town. The sidewalks were lined with tables piled high with merchandise and racks filled with clothes. Sifting among them were dozens of shoppers, mostly teenaged girls. Billy cruised slowly along until he spotted

Jess with Lisa sitting on a bench, talking. He'd
had a feeling he'd find them somewhere in town.
Now all he had to do was find Lisa's car.

There was a big public parking area behind
the shops on Main Street. There Billy found
Lisa's VW bug parked in a corner space. Billy
stopped his jeep behind it and got out. The bug's
engine compartment was unlocked and Billy
opened it and quickly disconnected the distrib-
utor cap. Then he got back into the jeep and
parked a row away. There was nothing to do
now except listen to the radio, have a cigarette,
and wait.

After a brief rest on the bench, Jess and Lisa
went to The Gap, the one store where they knew
they could find something they could afford. Jess
found a pair of jeans and Lisa got a hooded blue
BUM sweatshirt. Even with everything on sale,
the prices had gotten so high in Far Hampton
that the girls could only afford to get one item
apiece.

"I don't understand why I wanted to shop at
that sale," Lisa said as they walked through the
public parking lot behind Main Street. "Everything's still so expensive that I'd be better off
shopping at Caldor's."

"But this is the only chance we ever get to

shop on Main Street," Jess reminded her. "So we *have* to do it."

They reached Lisa's VW and got in. "Well, I'm glad this sale only comes once a year," Lisa said. "If it happened any more often I'd probably go broke." She put her key in the ignition and turned it. The motor whined but the car's engine wouldn't start.

"What now?" Lisa asked, trying to start it again.

"Do you have enough gas?" Jess asked.

"I filled the tank this morning." Lisa tried the motor again. "God, that's weird. My father just fixed this thing." She was about to try starting it again when she saw something in her rearview mirror that made her freeze.

"Uh-oh," she whispered. "Trouble."

Jess turned around and looked out the back window. Billy Petersen was strolling toward them. Jess couldn't help remembering the last time she'd spoken to him. It was the night Gary had drowned. Earlier on that awful night, Billy had driven Jess out to the point. Jess had gone because she'd wanted to tape Billy confessing that he stole the radar and hid it on Reed's sailboat. But Billy had discovered her hidden tape recorder and taken it away. Then he left Jess alone at the point and drove off.

Now Billy stopped by the window of Lisa's VW and looked in.

"Hi, Lisa. Sounds like your car won't start."

"That's right," Lisa answered tersely.

"Maybe I could help," Billy offered.

"Thanks, Billy, but we can live without your help," Lisa replied coldly.

"Hey, be nice," Billy said.

"Why?" Lisa asked. "You weren't very nice to Jess."

Billy leaned lower so he could see Jess, sitting tight-lipped in the passenger seat. "I owe you a real apology, Jess. You know, I was drinking a lot and I did some stuff I'm really ashamed of now. I'm really sorry."

Jess gave him a brief nod and then looked away. He sounded sincere, but with Billy you never knew.

"Look," Billy said to Lisa. "Maybe I can give you a ride to a garage or something."

Lisa shook her head. "I can't afford to take this to a garage. My father always fixes it himself when something goes wrong."

"Well, then I'll call a tow truck for you," Billy said. "They'll tow it home."

"I can't pay for that, either," Lisa said. "I just spent all my money on clothes."

"Then I'll take you to call your father," Billy said.

"He's in the city all week working," Lisa said.

Jess glanced past Lisa at Billy. It was hard to believe he was still trying to figure out a way to help them. Usually the only person Billy wanted to help was himself.

"Okay, look," Billy said. "I've got one last idea. I've got a chain in the back of my jeep. I could hook your car up behind mine and tow you home."

"Would we have to get into the jeep?" Lisa asked.

"No, you'd have to stay in your car and steer," Billy said.

Lisa and Jess glanced at each other. They were both really hesitant about letting Billy help them, but what choice did they have?

Half an hour later, Billy pulled his jeep over in front of Lisa's house. Lisa's VW with Lisa and Jess inside it glided to a halt behind him. Billy got out and started to undo the chain from the front of Lisa's car.

"Guess I'll be taking the bus to work for the rest of the week." Lisa groaned as she got out. "Whatever's wrong, I just hope it isn't too expensive to fix."

"You never know with these old cars," Billy said as he threw the chain in the back of the jeep. "Well, that's it. I guess I'll see you guys around."

He started to get back into the jeep. Suddenly Jess realized she had no way to get back to her house from Lisa's. Her parents had told her earlier that they were going out that night.

"Wait, Billy," she said.

Billy looked up, surprised. "Yeah?"

Jess took a deep breath. She knew she was taking a risk, but she didn't see what choice she had. "Listen, Billy, I don't have a way to get home. Do you think you could give me a ride?"

Billy stared at her. Things were going better than he'd planned. He'd never expected to get Jess alone this soon. "Well, okay."

Lisa quickly pulled Jess aside. "Are you sure you know what you're doing?" she whispered.

"No," Jess whispered back. "But at least he hasn't been drinking." She walked toward the jeep.

"No tricks, Billy," she said.

Billy nodded. "No tricks, Jess."

Jess went around to the passenger seat and got in. She told Billy where she lived and he started to drive. For most of the way home, Billy was silent and didn't even glance at her. Jess even began to feel a little bad. If Billy had a problem with alcohol and was trying to reform, then it was mean to hold the things he'd done against him. Finally she turned to him.

"I see you on the beach sometimes," she said.

Billy smirked. "Yeah, looks like I went from the top of the heap to the bottom."

"How long do you have to do community service?" Jess asked.

"Until the end of the summer," Billy said.

"That's too bad."

To Jess's surprise, Billy shook his head. "Not really, Jess. I deserved it after what I did."

Billy pulled the jeep up in front of Jess's house. Jess was tempted to hop out and run inside, but there was one question she wanted to ask first.

"Why did you do it?" she asked. "I mean, why did you want to get Reed into so much trouble?"

Billy stared through the windshield for a moment, and then turned to her. "It's hard to explain, Jess. It's just that all my life Reed's always been the best and I've always been second best. Like I said before, I was drinking a lot and doing dumb things, and I guess I just decided it was time he got what he deserved."

"Why did you think he deserved to get in

trouble?" Jess asked. "I mean, was it just because you were jealous?"

Billy stared through the windshield into the dark and didn't answer.

"Billy?" Jess said.

"You don't want to know, Jess," he said, shaking his head.

But if there was some secret about Reed, Jess did want to know. "Why won't you tell me?"

"It doesn't matter, Jess," Billy said. "I heard you weren't seeing Reed anymore. So you have nothing to worry about."

Jess stared across the dark at him. Of course Billy had no idea that she was finding Reed hard to resist again. Nobody except Andy suspected that. "Billy, I think you owe it to me to tell me what you know."

Billy turned and stared back at her. For several long moments he didn't say anything. Then he shook his head. "You're not going to like it."

"Tell me, Billy."

Billy took a deep breath. "Okay, Jess. The first day we started lifeguarding this year, Reed gave me a ride to the beach because my jeep was in the shop. As we rode there he told me he was going to have four girls before the summer was over. I guess it just pissed me off because I knew he'd probably do it."

Jess stared back at him. "I have to be honest with you, Billy. I really don't believe that."

Billy shrugged. "Like I said, Jess. You're not involved with him anymore, so it doesn't matter anyway."

Instead of getting out of the jeep, Jess just sat there, staring out into the dark. *"The tissue theory,"* Andy had said. *"Use them once and throw them away."* Even Reed had asked her if she thought he was using her.

"Reed would never do that," Jess insisted.

Billy chuckled. "It's a good thing you never really got to know my brother, Jess."

If only he knew, Jess couldn't help thinking.

"Suppose I told Reed you said that about him?" she asked.

Billy just shrugged as if he didn't care. "Go ahead, Jess. It's not like he's going to admit it to you."

Jess still didn't believe him. It couldn't be true. It just couldn't be! She reached for the door and pushed it open. "Thanks for the ride, Billy," she said and started up the path.

"See you around, Jess," Billy said, and drove away.

Billy's story gnawed at Jess all evening. She was certain Billy had made it up. But why? What

did Billy have to gain? Finally it was almost time
to go to bed, but Jess knew her thoughts would
keep her up all night if she didn't do something.
She picked up the phone and called Lisa.

"Hello?"

"It's Jess, am I calling too late?"

"Are you serious?" Lisa asked. "I'm still
trying to find things to go with my new sweatshirt. Do you think I made a mistake?"

"How can anyone make a mistake buying a
sweatshirt?" Jess asked.

"I guess you're right," Lisa said. "So what's
up?"

"I have to talk to you about something," Jess
said. "But you have to swear you won't tell
anyone."

"Consider it done," Lisa said.

"You know how Billy drove me home
tonight?"

"That's right!" Lisa gasped. "He didn't try
anything, did he?"

"He was the total opposite," Jess said. "He
couldn't have been more of a gentleman if he
tried."

"Wow, talk about night and day," Lisa said.

"It looks like he's really trying to change,"
Jess said. "He told me a lot of his problems had
to do with drinking."

"Well, that's no surprise," Lisa said.

"But listen to this," Jess said. "He told me that Reed told him at the beginning of the summer that he was going to get four girls by September."

"What?"

"You heard me," Jess said. "He says Reed bragged he'd have four girls this summer."

"Wait a minute," Lisa said. "I don't care if Billy had problems with drinking or not. This is still Billy Petersen we're talking about. You don't really believe him, do you?"

"I don't think so," Jess said. "Well, let's put it this way. I don't want to believe him."

"In other words, you're calling me so I can tell you that you shouldn't believe him," Lisa guessed.

"Basically."

"It doesn't sound like Reed to me," Lisa said. "It just doesn't seem like the kind of thing he'd do."

"That's what I think," Jess said. Hearing Lisa agree with her made her feel better.

"Then what's the problem?" Lisa asked.

"I still can't figure out why Billy would make up something like that," Jess said.

"Wait a minute," Lisa said. "Remember what I just said. This is Billy Petersen we're talking about. I don't care how nice he was tonight. This is someone who's so low he'd even get his own brother into trouble if it helped his cause."

"But he doesn't know that anything's going on between Reed and me," Jess said. "I mean, I'm not even sure anything's going on. Billy had nothing to gain by telling me. I just don't get it."

"You want my absolute honest-to-God opinion?" Lisa asked. "Don't lose any sleep over it. It's August, Jess. If Reed were going to try and get four girls by September, he would have moved on by now."

SEVEN

As the week progressed, Jess found herself spending more and more time with Reed. Andy wasn't around and Billy's story quickly faded from her thoughts. Still, Jess was being careful. It wasn't like she and Reed were starting to see each other again. Instead they just kept running into each other at the lifeguard shack and on the snack line. Toward the end of the week, they started to take their lunch breaks together.

"Doing anything after work today?" Reed asked one afternoon as they left the snack bar.

Jess stopped in the sand and looked at him. All week she'd felt the attraction between them growing and deepening. She'd begun to sense that it was only a matter of time until she and Reed got back together. But so far they'd just seen each other at work. This was the first time Reed had actually broached the subject of them doing something outside of work. At least, that was what she suspected he was going to suggest.

"No," she said. "Why?"

"It's going to be a nice evening," Reed said. "There's a good breeze. I thought I'd take a sail. Want to come?"

Jess looked down at the sand. The memory of the last time she was with him on *Simplicity* came back to her. That rainy afternoon they'd spent together in the cabin, locked in each other's arms. Jess couldn't deny that she yearned to feel those arms again. She shook the thought away and gazed down the beach at the long curling sets of waves rolling in toward the shore.

"I don't know, Reed," Jess said. "I'm not sure I'm ready for that."

"Sailing?" Reed looked surprised.

"Not that," Jess said. "The other part."

Reed nodded as if he understood. "I wasn't suggesting anything except sailing, Jess."

Jess looked up and gazed into his handsome dark eyes. She knew she wasn't going to say no.

The sky was deep blue and cloudless. With her taut white sails filled with wind, *Simplicity* cut through the waves. Wearing a gray St. Peter's sweatshirt, his brown hair dancing in the wind, Reed sat in the back of the cockpit with one hand on the rudder. Jess sat across from him, her hands on the railing to steady herself, her hair tucked under a white St. Peter's baseball cap.

"Ever been sailing before?" Reed asked.

"A few times," Jess said.

"Did you like it?"

"It's hard to say," Jess replied. "The first time I went there was no wind. The second time it was really foggy."

"Then you've never been out on a day like this," Reed said.

Jess shook her head. A few long strands of blonde hair had worked their way out from under the baseball cap and fluttered in the breeze.

"I don't know what we're going to do about your hair," Reed said.

"Why?" Jess asked.

"It's too long for sailing."

"I can just keep it tucked in," Jess said, grabbing the loose strands and tucking them under the hat.

"But it always comes out," Reed said. "It's okay on a day like today. But if you're in any kind of rough weather it could really be a problem."

"Just because it gets loose?" Jess asked, puzzled.

"You don't want to get it tangled in the ropes or caught in a winch," Reed said.

"Then I just won't go sailing in bad weather," Jess said.

"It could happen in *any* weather," Reed said. The next thing Jess knew, he pulled out a short piece of cord and clamped it between his teeth. Then he slid forward and reached for her hair.

"What are you doing?" Jess asked.

"Turn away," Reed said through his clenched teeth.

Jess turned and felt his fingers slide through her hair and pull it back.

"I didn't bring a rubber band," she said.

"That's why they teach knots in sailing," Reed replied. She felt him smooth her hair back carefully. His touch sent goose bumps across her shoulders. How easy it would be to simply lean back and be enveloped in his arms.

"There." Reed finished tying her hair back and let go. Then he turned to look back at the thin strip of beach behind them.

"Prepare to come about," he said, pulling the rudder around.

Jess knew this meant it was time to duck as the boom swung over them. A moment later the sailboat changed direction. Jess admired Reed's ability to control *Simplicity*. He seemed so confident and comfortable at the helm.

"Jess," Reed said, pointing to a rope. "Free the jib line from the cleat."

"How do I do it?" Jess asked.

"Just pull up on it and let go."

Jess got up and carefully crossed toward the line. She gave it a pull and it shot out of her hands. Now the jib, the small sail in front of the large main sail, started to flap noisily in the wind.

"Now grab that rope and pull it in on the other side," Reed said, pointing at another rope.

Jess crossed the cockpit, picked the rope and pulled. The jib came across the mast and started to tighten.

"Now secure the rope in the cleat," Reed said.

"How?" Jess asked.

"Just pull it down between the teeth."

Teeth? Jess stared down at what she thought was the cleat and didn't see any teeth.

"Here you go." The next thing she knew, Reed came up beside her. He took the rope and jammed it into something other than what she thought was the cleat.

"Like that," Reed said, straightening up and facing her.

Suddenly Jess had a startling thought. "Who's steering the boat?"

"I tied off the rudder," Reed said, pointing at

the stern. Jess saw a heavy piece of rope holding the rudder still.

"Is that safe?" she asked.

"Sure," Reed said with a smile. "As long as — "

Before he could finish the sentence, the boat suddenly tilted.

"Look out!" Reed shouted and grabbed Jess, pulling her to the cockpit floor. A second later the boom swung across the cockpit. Jess lay on the floor in Reed's arms. She knew if she'd still been standing the boom would have hit her in the head.

"That was close," Reed said.

Jess turned and looked at him. She was lying in his arms, their faces were only inches apart.

"I asked you if it was safe," she said. "You started to say as long as . . ."

"As long as the wind doesn't shift," Reed said.

"The wind shifted, didn't it?" Jess said.

Reed nodded. He was gazing into her eyes. Jess felt his arms tighten around her. Reed moved his face closer. Jess felt her own arms tighten around his body, pulling him toward her. A second later they kissed.

Their kisses became passionate. Jess felt Reed's hot breath on her neck and ears. She felt his warm body as she slid her hands under his sweatshirt. The floor was hard, but she didn't care. Reed's hands caressed her, his face brushed against her cheek. Nothing else mattered. . . .

The sailboat suddenly tilted again. Still locked in each other's arms, Jess and Reed rolled over. The next thing Jess knew, she was lying on top of him.

"I guess the wind shifted again," Jess said with a smile.

Beneath her, Reed nodded. "I hate to say it, but if I don't take over the helm pretty soon we'll probably wind up in the middle of the ocean."

"I thought that's what you wanted," Jess said playfully.

"Uh, sure, but not this evening," Reed said.

"Couldn't we just radio for help?" Jess asked, half-serious.

"Normally, yes," Reed said. "But my radio's being fixed."

He got up slowly and helped Jess to her feet. Reed sat back in the stern again, but this time Jess sat with him. Reed put one arm around her shoulders and pulled her close while he steered with the other arm. The wind was in Jess's face and she let her head lean back into the crook of his neck. They sailed that way for the rest of the evening.

"So how'd you like it?" Reed asked. He'd driven her home after sailing and now they were sitting in his jeep, parked outside her house.

"It's fun, as long as you don't get clobbered by the boom," Jess said.

"It keeps you on your toes," Reed said with a smile.

Jess smiled back at him. The sun was setting and the sky above them was turning dark. The few clouds were almost crimson as the red sun started to disappear. But Reed wasn't looking at the clouds. He was gazing at her.

"I think you've got the makings of a good sailor," he said.

"Oh, I bet you say that to all the girls," Jess replied. She was mostly teasing, but not entirely.

"Oh, yeah." Reed grinned. "I take three or four dates a week out on *Simplicity*. In fact, I'm thinking of renaming her *The Love Boat*."

"So, do you still plan to sail across the ocean next summer?" she said.

"Sure do," Reed said with a nod.

"I thought you said you'd need a lot of time to prepare," Jess said.

Reed nodded. A few weeks earlier he'd told Jess that he wouldn't be able to sail much once he went back to do senior year at St. Peter's Prep.

"Guess I'll have to figure out some way to do it," he said.

Jess knew she was hoping Reed would say he wasn't going back to prep school for senior year. More than anything, that was what she wished for. But it was an impossible dream. St. Peter's Prep was one of the best schools in the country, especially compared to Far Hampton High where barely half the graduating class even went on to college.

Jess felt a little sad. Lisa had talked about the possibility of a long-distance relationship, but Jess still didn't believe it was possible.

"You're going to the party tomorrow night, aren't you?" Reed's voice snapped her out of her thoughts.

"It's my mom's birthday and Dad and I are taking her out to dinner," she said. "But I should be able to get there on time."

Reed reached across the seat and ran his hand through her long blonde hair. Jess felt his fingers touch her ear. It sent a thrill through her.

"It's not that late," Reed said. "Maybe we could take a ride."

Jess was so tempted. But they were already parked in front of her house and she'd seen her mother part the kitchen curtains and look out at them. If they left and went somewhere now, her mother might ask questions when she got home later.

"Not now," Jess said, taking his hand and squeezing it. "Let's wait. Until the party."

Jess wasn't the only one who couldn't wait until the party. Neither could Billy. As the sun set, he waited near the entrance to the Far Hampton Marina for Paula to arrive. Just past the entrance to the marina, dozens of sailboats and cabin cruisers were lined up along the docks.

Billy saw Paula's car pull into the marina. Paula got out and walked toward him.

"Why did you call me and tell me to meet you here?" she asked uncomfortably. "What's going on, Billy?"

"I've decided I know what you can do for me," Billy said.

Paula looked around. "Here?"

"Yeah, come on." Billy picked up a black bag and led her out onto the dock. They started to walk past the cabin cruisers and sailboats.

"I'd really appreciate it if you'd tell me what's going on," Paula said as she followed him.

"You'll see," Billy said. Toward the end of the dock they came to a cabin cruiser named the *Gaila*. Billy stepped over the transom and turned back to Paula, offering his hand. Paula hesitated.

"Whose boat is this?" she asked.

"My father's," Billy replied.

Paula eyes him suspiciously. "Reed never told me your father had a boat like this."

"Reed never told you a lot of things," Billy said, holding out his hand for her. "My old man used to use it for business entertaining. But it's named after my mother and when she died he pretty much stopped using it. Now come on."

Paula sighed and stepped over the transom and into the back of the boat beside Billy. She thought she had a pretty good idea of what was going to come next.

"You swear if I do what you want you'll give me that tape?" Paula asked.

"I swear, Paula," Billy said.

A glass sliding door led from the back of the boat into the main cabin, but instead of going in, Billy slid his hand under the boat's starboard railing and started to feel for something.

"What are you doing?" Paula asked.

"Looking for a key," Billy replied.

"What? I thought you said this was your father's boat," Paula said nervously. "Look, Billy, I don't know what you've got planned, but I'm not going to help you break the law."

"Just keep your voice down, okay?" Billy said

as he moved over to the port railing and started to feel under it.

"I'm serious, Billy," Paula said.

"There!" Billy stood up and held out a key. "Isn't it amazing how everyone leaves a spare key?" He picked up the black bag and used the key to open the sliding glass door. A moment later he stepped into the cabin and flicked on a light.

Paula remained outside.

"Well, come on," Billy said.

"No." Paula shook her head. "I'll do what you want, Billy, as long as it doesn't involve breaking and entering."

"I told you, this is my father's boat," Billy said.

"Then how come you had to look for the key?" Paula asked.

"Because I'm not allowed to use it, okay?" Billy said. "But it's not like my old man's going to send me to jail if I get caught."

But Paula still hesitated. She couldn't stand the thought of what was coming.

"Well?" Billy asked impatiently.

"What if someone catches us?" Paula asked.

"No one's going to catch us," Billy said. "Now come on."

But Paula didn't move.

"Hey, listen," Billy said. "I've made two copies of that tape. If you don't get your butt in here right now, one copy's going to Chief Sloat first thing in the morning and the other's going to Reed."

Paula sighed. She really had to have that tape. She stepped into the room inside, the salon. It reminded her of a small living room. There was a couch against one wall and a wooden dining table against the other.

At the far end of the salon, Billy stepped down through a varnished wooden door into a small hallway. To his left was the boat's galley. To his right was the bathroom. Ahead was another door. Billy pushed it open and reached inside for a light switch.

"Perfect!" Billy mumbled as the lights burst on. He stepped into the stateroom. Paula stopped in the doorway and stared in, feeling ill. On either side of the room, a set of double-decker bunks was built into the wall. It was so obvious what Billy had in mind. Never in her life had she thought she'd lower herself to this.

"Sit on that bunk," Billy ordered, pointing to the lower bunk on the left.

Paula recoiled at the thought of what was going to come next. "Wait, Billy. You know how I offered you five hundred dollars the other day? I'll double it. I'll give you a thousand for those tapes."

"Just sit down," Billy growled.

Paula shrugged and sat down. It was obvious Billy didn't care about the money. That was the problem with rich people. You couldn't buy them off.

Meanwhile Billy opened his black bag and took out the small video camera with the wide angle lens he'd shown her in his room the other night.

"Oh, no, Billy," she gasped and started to get up. "There's no way. I don't care what you do with those tapes — "

"Just shut up and sit down," Billy snapped.

"No, Billy, I won't!" Paula made a run for the door, but Billy grabbed her and threw her back onto the bunk so hard that she banged her knee.

"You hurt me!" she cried out.

"That's nothing compared to what I'll do if you don't chill out," Billy threatened.

Paula sat on the bed and didn't move. She was trapped.

Meanwhile, Billy placed the camera in the corner of the upper bunk opposite the one she was sitting on. He fiddled with it for a few moments until he had it aimed correctly.

"Why are you doing this?" Paula asked.

"You'll see," Billy said.

"You said if I cooperated you were going to *give* me the tape, not make a new one."

"That's right," Billy said. He turned off the camera's automatic focus and adjusted the lens so that everything would be slightly blurry.

"Okay, come here," he said.

"No," Paula said.

Billy turned and glared at her. "You don't even know what I'm doing. But if you don't come here right now, I'll do what you *think* I'm going to do."

Paula stood up and stepped toward him. Billy took her hand and let her feel the camera.

"You feel the button?" he asked. "That turns the camera on. I've got a one-hour tape in there so you should have plenty of time."

"Time for what?" Paula asked, now totally confused.

"Time to turn it on before you get Reed down here," Billy said.

"What are you talking about?" Paula asked.

"You're going to get my brother down here," Billy said. "You'll want him to sit facing the camera. Then you'll sit down with your back to it."

"When?" Paula asked. None of this made any sense to her.

"Tomorrow night the lifeguards are having a party on this boat," Billy said. "Somehow you're going to get Reed down here, *and* you're going to borrow Lisa's denim jacket. The one with the rose on the back. Try to keep your back to the camera as much as possible. You're about the same size as Lisa and you both have dark hair. I've got the camera just enough out of focus so that it should be real hard to tell on tape that it's you and not Lisa."

Paula nodded. It was obvious that Billy wanted her to pretend she was Lisa. "What do I do with Reed once I get him down here?"

"Put the moves on him," Billy said.

Paula was shocked. "Why?"

"You want Reed back, don't you?" Billy asked. "Well, if you're lucky, you may just get your wish."

Paula stared at him in amazement. "Are you serious?"

Billy nodded. "And unlike you, when I say I'm going to try to get someone for you, I mean it."

The next night, Lisa and Reed lugged a big Styrofoam cooler filled with drinks down the dock and onto the *Gaila*. After a week of incredible heat, the weather had suddenly turned unusually cool. Lisa thought it would be a nice evening for a party. She had planned to ask Andy to help them set up, but he'd called from New Hampshire that morning and said he wouldn't be able to make it home for the party because his aunt had broken her ankle and they had to take her to the hospital that day.

Lisa was very disappointed. She'd seen how Jess and Reed had been getting closer all week, and she'd hoped that when Andy saw them together at the party he'd give up on his quest to make Jess his.

"You think we should put this inside or out here on the deck?" Reed asked, pointing at the cooler.

"Uh, let's put some in the fridge and leave some out here," Lisa said. "It's supposed to be a nice cool evening, and after all this hot weather recently I think people may want to stay outside."

Reed slid the cooler off to the side. "I'll go back to the car and get the rest of the stuff."

"Want me to come?" Lisa asked.

"No, I can handle it myself."

Lisa watched him jog back toward her car. She recalled what Jess had told her Billy had said about Reed wanting four girls that summer. No, it just didn't seem possible. He just wasn't that kind of guy.

Lisa wasn't the only person who watched Reed go down the dock toward the car. One dock away, crouching between two sailboats, Paula was also watching. Billy had given her an almost impossible task. Somehow she had to get Reed alone downstairs in the boat and pretend to be Lisa. Paula had spent hours trying to figure out how to do it. Finally, she'd come up with a plan.

Wearing an old pair of jeans and a T-shirt she didn't care about, Paula jumped off the dock and into the harbor. On the dock, Reed was walking back toward the *Gaila,* carrying Lisa's portable CD player and a brown grocery bag filled with snacks.

"Reed!" Paula cried and swam toward him.

Reed stopped and stared at her. His jaw dropped. "Paula! What are you doing in the water?"

Paula swam toward the dock. Reed quickly put down the CD player and bag and helped her out of the harbor.

"Oh, Reed," she gasped as he pulled her soaking wet onto the dock. "You won't believe what happened."

"Are you okay?" Reed asked with a bewildered look on his face.

"Yes, I think so." Paula stood dripping on the dock and wrapped her arms around herself. "But I'm freezing."

"Well, come on, I'll get you dry," Reed said.

As he led her toward the *Gaila*, Paula told him how she'd gone to the Salty Dog bar an hour ago to hang out and was picked up by a guy who invited her back to his boat.

"Did you know him?" Reed asked.

"No." Paula shook her head. "But he seemed nice at the time."

Reed rolled his eyes. "I bet."

They got to the *Gaila*. "Paula!" Lisa gasped. "What happened to you?"

"It's a long story," Paula said, turning to Reed. "Is there some place I could dry off?"

"Of course," Reed said. "Come on."

Just as Paula had hoped, Reed led her through the cabin and down to the bathroom where he gave her some towels. Paula closed the bathroom door, stripped down to her underwear, and dried off the best she could. Then she opened the door a hair.

"Does Lisa have anything dry I could wear?" Paula asked.

"I'll go ask," Reed said, going back up to the

cabin. As soon as he was gone, Paula dashed out of the bathroom and into the stateroom. She quickly reached up to the video camera on the top bunk and switched it on. Then she went back into the bathroom.

A few moments later Reed returned with Lisa's denim jacket. "Lisa said you could use this," he said, handing it through the doorway to her.

Paula smiled and slipped it on. "Thanks."

"Do you want me to take you back to your house?" Reed asked.

"Oh, God, no!" Paula gasped. "I can't go back there. I told my parents I was going with a friend to the movies. If they found out I met a guy in a bar, they'll kill me."

Now Lisa came down from the salon.

"Paula needs some dry clothes," Reed said.

"Hmmm." Lisa rubbed her chin.

Inside the bathroom, Paula could just imagine what Lisa was thinking. Probably trying to figure out how she could help her, but at the same time get rid of her before the party began.

"Well, you and I are almost the same size," Lisa said. "Tell you what. Let me run home and get you some things to wear. Then you could take your wet things to the laundromat in town and get them dried before you go home."

"Oh, would you?" Paula gasped gratefully.

"Sure," Lisa said. "Just wait here. I'll be back in twenty minutes."

Through the crack in the bathroom doorway, Paula watched Lisa go back up the stairs and out of the cabin. Maybe her plan would work after all!

As soon as Lisa was gone, Paula pushed open the bathroom door and came out. Reed looked a little surprised to see her dressed only in Lisa's denim jacket.

"Don't worry," Paula said. "I've still got my underwear on. Have you got a comb?"

"Uh, sure." Reed reached into his back pocket and gave her one. Paula used it to comb out her wet hair. Combed straight, it looked a lot like Lisa's, only longer. But Paula knew she could tuck it inside the collar of the denim jacket. Then it would look like it was the same length. Now she had to get Reed into the stateroom.

"It's kind of cold out," Paula said, pretending to shiver. "Is there somewhere warm I could wait?"

"Well, there's the stateroom," Reed said, pushing open the door.

Paula went in and sat down on the bunk Billy had told her to sit on so that her back would face the camera. Reed looked around awkwardly and then leaned against the bunk opposite her. Paula knew she'd have to get him to sit, but she couldn't rush things.

"I'm really sorry to do this to you, Reed," she said.

"Why would you go to a place like the Salty Dog?" Reed asked.

Paula shrugged. "A lot of college guys hang out there. I thought maybe I could meet one."

Reed frowned. "And why did you agree to go back to that guy's boat?"

Paula pretended to be both annoyed and embarrassed by the questions. "I told you, Reed. He seemed nice. It wasn't until we got to his boat that I realized what was going on."

"What *was* going on?" Reed asked.

"There were two more guys on the boat," Paula said. "The guy I met, he said his name was Ted, promised me we'd stay at the dock. But after he had a few drinks he said he wanted to go for a cruise. That's when I got worried. I mean, the last thing I wanted to do was go out in a boat with three strange guys drinking beer."

"So what happened?" Reed asked.

"I told them I didn't want to go, but then Ted and his friends started to threaten me," Paula said, pretending to shiver at the memory. "The next thing I knew, Ted started the boat and headed out of the harbor. By then I knew what they had in mind so I waited until they'd turned their backs and then jumped out into the harbor."

"What did the guys do?" Reed asked.

"They just kept going," Paula said.

Reed was quiet for a moment and Paula worried that he'd thought of something about her story that didn't make sense.

"What is it?" she asked, trying to hide her nervousness.

"Well, nothing," Reed said with a shrug. "I just don't remember seeing any boats heading out of the harbor before."

"Maybe you missed it," Paula said.

Reed nodded. He seemed to have other things on his mind. "I just don't get it, Paula," he said. "I mean, why in the world would you go with some stranger on his boat?"

Paula knew this was her opportunity. She reached up and gestured for Reed to sit down on the bunk with her. "Because I was lonely, Reed. Ever since you and I broke up, nobody wants to be my friend. I can't find any decent guys to go out with. . . . The truth is, I don't really want to go out with anyone else."

Paula had planned to force tears out of her

eyes, but they came much more easily than she'd expected. "I used to have the most handsome boyfriend in Far Hampton," she said with a sniff. "Now I've got no one."

She leaned toward Reed and he took her into his arms to comfort her. "I miss you so much, Reed," she whispered, reaching up and feeling his face with her hands. "Don't you ever think about me anymore?"

Paula slid her arms around his neck and slowly pulled him down into a kiss. Somewhere in the last few moments the act had ended. Paula wasn't kissing Reed for the camera, she was kissing him for herself. She was surprised that Reed let her kiss him. She wondered if he was filled with guilt over seeing her so unhappy. Or maybe it was just possible that he still harbored some feelings for her. . . .

But then he pulled away.

"No, Paula," he said.

"You sure, Reed?" Paula whispered pleadingly, still holding him close. "Couldn't it ever be the way it used to be?"

"I don't think so, Paula," Reed said. "I'm sorry."

Paula bowed her head. She'd done what she'd done to fulfill her part of the deal with Billy. But the truth was, she'd realized her feelings for

Reed were stronger than ever. All she really wanted was for Reed to kiss her and hold her in his arms.

With a pair of jeans and a sweatshirt in hand, Lisa jogged down the dock and climbed aboard the *Gaila*. She thought it would be best if Paula changed clothes and left before the others arrived, especially Jess. If Jess saw Paula and Reed there, it might give her the wrong idea.

"Reed? Paula?" Lisa entered the salon and looked around for them. That was weird. Where could they be? Puzzled, Lisa went down toward the bathroom. That was empty, too. So where else? The stateroom door was closed. Without thinking, Lisa pushed it open.

"Oops! Sorry!" Lisa quickly backed out of the room and closed the door. She couldn't believe what she'd stumbled into. Reed and Paula were sitting on one of the bunks with their arms around each other!

A second later the door swung open and Reed stood there. "It's okay, Lisa," he said calmly. "Paula and I were just talking. Did you bring the clothes?"

Lisa nodded quietly and handed them to him. It sure looked to her like they were doing more than talking.

*   *   *

A little while later Reed gave Paula a ride to the laundromat so that she could wash and dry her clothes.

"It's been a long time since I sat in this jeep," Paula said as Reed drove toward town.

"You never used to like it," Reed said. "Remember? You always complained that your hair got blown around too much."

Paula knew he was right. How could she explain that she'd changed? Or rather, that she would change if it meant having Reed back?

"Maybe I didn't appreciate it then," she said.

Reed glanced at her and gave her a skeptical look. "And you do now?"

"I appreciate what went along with riding in this jeep," Paula said.

Reed was quiet for the rest of the ride. They drove into town and parked outside the laundromat, but Paula was reluctant to get out of the jeep.

"You sure you have to go back to the party?" she asked, filled with hope that he'd stay with her instead.

"I'm *giving* the party," Reed said. "I have to go back."

"It's because Jess is going to be there, isn't it?" Paula asked.

Reed didn't answer. Paula glanced in at the brightly lit laundromat. A woman wearing hair curlers and smoking a cigarette was reading the *Ladies Home Journal*.

"Would you ever have imagined me sitting in a laundromat doing clothes?" Paula asked with a sigh.

Reed turned and looked at her. "I don't get it, Paula. The next thing I know, you'll start telling me how much you miss sailing."

"I miss *you*, Reed," Paula said.

"I'm sure you can find another stud to show off at the beach and the dance clubs," Reed said.

"Maybe I've figured out that I don't want that anymore," Paula said.

"Oh?" Reed raised an eyebrow. "And what do you want?"

"Somebody who cares about me," Paula said. "And somebody I care about. We were together for a long time, Reed. I know we felt that way about each other once."

Reed nodded. "A lot of things have changed since then, Paula."

"I know," Paula said. "I acted stupid and superficial. But I realize that now. And I know you've met someone new, but you've only known her for a month. You've known me for years. That has to count for something."

Reed gazed away down the street. Paula realized he was actually listening and considering what she said. Maybe his feelings for Jess weren't as strong as she thought! Her heart began to fill with hope.

"Reed?" she said.

He shook his head. "I'm sorry, Paula, I've got to get back to the party."

He started his jeep and drove away into the night. Paula stood on the corner outside the laundromat and watched him go. Suddenly she found herself wishing with all her heart that Billy's plan would work.

Normally Jess didn't like to arrive at parties early. Everyone tended to be stiff and awkward. It usually took a crowd to get them to relax. But tonight Jess couldn't wait. She just wanted to see Reed so much, she'd even gotten her parents to end her mom's birthday dinner a little early.

As she walked down the dock toward the *Gaila,* she could see Lisa in the back of the cabin cruiser, setting up her CD player. As Jess stepped onto the transom, Lisa straightened up with a surprised look on her face.

"Jess!" she gasped.

"I know I'm early," Jess said, looking around. "Where's Reed?"

"Uh, he had to, uh, go into town to get something," Lisa stammered nervously.

Jess didn't understand why her friend was acting that way. "Is something wrong?"

"Wrong? Oh, no," Lisa said. "I'm sure Reed will be back any minute now."

Jess stared at her. Lisa was definitely acting weird. "Are you *sure* something isn't wrong?"

"Positive," Lisa said. "It's just pre-party jitters."

By the time Reed got back to the party, Jess was there along with Ellie and Stu and a few of their friends. Lisa's portable CD player was playing music and people were drinking and talking loudly.

"I thought I was going to be the late one," Jess teased him as he got a Coke out of the cooler.

"Something came up," Reed replied vaguely.

"Lisa said you had to go into town to get something," Jess said.

"Uh, yeah." Reed nodded.

"What was it?" Jess asked.

"It's not important," Reed said.

Jess frowned. She didn't understand why Reed was suddenly acting so vague. Sometimes she felt so close to him. Then he'd do something like this and she'd feel like he was a million miles away.

"Want to go up to the bow?" Reed asked.

"Why?" Jess asked.

"Might be a little quieter."

Jess hesitated. "I don't know, Reed. I mean, it seems like you have all these secrets. . . ."

Reed turned and looked deep into her eyes. "You have to believe me when I tell you it wasn't important, Jess. Really. The only thing that's important to me is that we're together."

Jess felt her resistance melt away. She knew she wanted to be with him. Besides, there was no law that said he couldn't have a secret.

"Okay," she said.

Reed took her hand and they walked along the side of the cabin cruiser to the foredeck and the bow. A low stainless-steel rail ran along the edge of the bow and they sat down and let their feet dangle over the side of the hull. The moon was just a sliver in the dark sky and a slight cool breeze blew into their faces as they stared out at the lights of the marina.

"I'm glad that heat wave finally broke," Jess said.

"Sounds like the weather's going to be nice for the next few days," Reed said.

"That'll be a relief," Jess said.

Reed was quiet for a moment. Jess wondered if he was trying to think of something to talk about other than the weather. She could feel the excitement of being with him. She was keenly aware of his slightest movement, of the most minute change in the tone of his voice.

"So how are you?" Reed asked.

"Okay, I guess," Jess said.

"Feeling a little better these days?"

"A little."

"I'm really sorry we had to go through all that, Jess," Reed said. "But the truth is, I think we just had a run of really bad luck. It shouldn't stop us from picking up where we left off."

Jess turned and looked in his face searchingly. "You think?"

Reed nodded. "Yes, that's what I think. I'm not saying you should never look back, but you have to look ahead a little, too."

"And when you look ahead, what do you see?" Jess asked.

Reed stared out into the marina. "Well, I see . . . a dock and some boats and a couple of sleeping sea gulls."

"That's not what I meant!" Jess grinned and gave him a playful nudge. "I meant, when you look ahead into your future."

Reed smiled back. "I know what you meant.

So what do I see? I see a beautiful girl with long blonde hair flowing out behind her."

"What month is it?" Jess asked.

"Hmmm." Reed rubbed his chin. "July."

"But it's August now," Jess said. "I thought we weren't looking back."

"I'm not," Reed said with a smile.

"You're talking about *next* July?" Jess asked. Reed nodded.

"And where is this girl?" Jess asked.

"She's sitting on the bow of *Simplicity* with her face in the wind," Reed said.

"And where is *Simplicity*?" Jess asked.

"Oh . . ." Reed scratched his head. "I'd say about halfway across the Atlantic at that point."

Jess stared at him. "You'd want me to go with you?"

"If you want to come," Reed said.

"But I don't even know how to sail."

"That's not true," Reed said. "You know how to pull the jib line in."

"But there's so much more to learn," Jess said.

"Then I'll teach it to you," said Reed.

"But when?" Jess asked. "The summer's more than half over."

"We've still got this fall and next spring," Reed said.

"But I thought you were going back to prep school," Jess said.

"Nothing's etched in stone, Jess," Reed said. "Believe me."

Jess stared at him wide-eyed. She understood what he was saying. He wanted to be with her this summer, then in the fall and spring and next summer. Suddenly very little else in her life seemed to matter. Reed looked back at her, then drew her toward him for a kiss.

The party ended and Reed and Jess drove back to the Petersen estate. Reed drove in through the gates and then over to the dock and got out of the jeep.

"Wait here," he whispered and kissed her softly.

Jess waited while Reed walked out onto the dock and went into his sailboat. Moments later he returned with a blanket.

They drove back to the garage beside the mansion and got out. Hand in hand they walked out onto the private beach. The sand was cool beneath their feet. Reed spread out the blanket and they lay down on it.

The sky was a sheet of black speckled with twinkling stars, the moon just a curving sliver as thin as a feather seen sideways. Jess felt Reed's weight on her, enveloping and protecting her from the cool night air. She felt his lips on her ears and neck and mouth. She slid her hands inside his shirt. His back felt warm and smooth. A shooting star streaked across the sky and Jess caught her breath as Reed's hands slid gently over her. Jess held on tight, breathing hotly into his ear, sliding her fingers through his thick long hair. She wanted this moment to last forever.

EIGHT

The next day Jess was awakened by a knock on her bedroom door. She opened her eyes and rubbed them as she watched her mother poke her head in.

"Are you okay, hon?" Mrs. Sloat asked.

"Uh, sure, why?" Jess asked.

"Because it's one o'clock in the afternoon. I don't think I've ever seen you sleep this late before."

"Guess I was just tired, Mom," Jess replied, not feeling it necessary to explain that she hadn't gotten home until five A.M.

"Well, all right," her mother said. "As long as you're not sick."

"I'm not, Mom," Jess said. "I just needed to catch up on my sleep."

"Okay. And by the way, I found this outside the front door this morning," her mother said, holding up a thick Manila envelope. "It's addressed to you. Someone must have left it."

Jess nodded and didn't think much about it. Her thoughts immediately flew back to the night before and Reed. They'd spent the night together under the stars, locked in an unending embrace. He'd said he wanted to see her all fall, all spring, and next summer! Jess felt like singing, or flying, or shouting for joy.

Later, after she took a shower and came back to her room to get dressed, she noticed the Manila envelope her mother had left on her desk. Someone had printed *Jess Sloat* on the outside. But there was no return address or indication of where it had come from. Jess opened it and a videocassette slipped out. The tape bore no markings.

Very strange, Jess thought.

After she got dressed, Jess took the tape into the den and slid it into the VCR. For a few moments, all she saw was gray-and-white static. Jess yawned. She couldn't imagine what this was about. Then a fuzzy grayish picture appeared on the screen. It looked like the kind of picture she'd seen on security monitors in stores. There were two people in the picture, sitting close together on some kind of bunk.

Oh my God! The shock of recognition hit Jess like a slap in the face. Suddenly she was staring wide-eyed at the television. It was Reed and Lisa! Lisa had her back to the camera, and except for the denim jacket with the rose on the back, she didn't appear to be wearing any clothes! Jess watched in total amazement as Lisa reached toward Reed and drew him into a kiss.

The screen went to static again. Jess quickly rewound the tape and replayed it. It had to be a trick. It couldn't really be Reed! But despite the fuzziness of the focus, there was no doubt that it was Reed.

Jess felt the blood drain out of her face and a sickening knot build in her stomach.

He said he'd have four girls before the end of the summer. . . .

Jess played the tape again, but she was beginning to feel weak and dizzy. This couldn't be happening. Not after last night. Not after all the things Reed said . . . and did . . .

The tape ended. Tears started to stream out of Jess's eyes. She felt as if someone or something were trying to rip her heart out of her chest. She pulled the tape out of the VCR and stumbled back toward her room and locked the door.

Inside she threw herself on the bed and buried her face in a pillow. Reed had lied to her. All that talk about spending the fall and spring together, about sailing to Europe next summer . . . it was all just lies and promises designed to get her to drop her guard so that he could get what he wanted.

And what about Lisa? Jess had been with Reed until five in the morning. That meant the tape must have been made before then. Suddenly Jess sat up. No wonder Lisa had acted so strange when Jess first got to the party! She wasn't acting strange, she was acting guilty!

So, while pretending to be a totally innocent friend, Lisa had actually been trying to steal her boyfriend.

And to Reed she was nothing but a number on a scorecard.

Once again Jess threw herself down on her bed. She wanted to be alone.

Forever.

Jess lay on her bed with a pillow pulled over her head. She heard the faint sound of a telephone ringing, but made no effort to answer it.

Soon there was a knock on her door.

"Jess?" It was her mother.

"What?"

"Phone for you."

"I don't want to talk," Jess said.

"But you don't even know who it is," her mother said through the door.

"It doesn't matter."

"It's Lisa, hon," Mrs. Sloat said. "Is something wrong?"

Jess couldn't imagine why Lisa would be calling, unless it was to brag that she was trying to steal Reed.

"Should I tell Lisa you'll call her back?"

"Sure, Mom," Jess said weakly.

"Hon, are you sure you're okay?" her mother said. "You don't sound well."

"I just want to be alone," Jess said.

The hours passed. Jess turned off the lights and kept the shades drawn. She wondered briefly who had left the tape for her. Obviously it was someone who wanted her to know the truth. Andy? Paula? It could have been anyone. And it didn't matter anyway. The only thing that mattered was what was on the tape. Jess stared at the ceiling. The dimness of her room reflected the darkness in her heart. Each time she thought of Reed, she cried. She couldn't believe how he'd used her.

At least once an hour her mother knocked and asked if there was anything she could do. But there was nothing anyone could do. Jess knew she'd been used and betrayed. She felt hollow and devastated.

There was another knock on the door.

"Please leave me alone, Mom," Jess said. "I'll come out when I'm ready."

"It's not Mom," a voice said.

It was Andy!

Jess sat up on the bed. She knew she must have looked like a mess. Her eyes felt puffy and she hadn't bothered to put on any makeup. Could she let Andy in? How could she refuse? But how could she tell him what had happened? She knew how he'd react. He'd say, *"I told you so."* He'd warned her that Reed was no good for her and she hadn't listened. Jess knew Andy would be furious at her. He might even turn around and walk right back out.

And she couldn't let that happen. Now that Lisa and Reed had betrayed her, Andy was the only friend she had left.

"Jess?" Andy said through the door.

"Uh, give me a moment, Andy." Jess sat up on her bed and turned on the light. She went around the room and opened the shades to let the sunlight in. She picked up her clothes from the night before and quickly made her bed.

"Am I allowed in yet?" Andy asked.

"Soon," Jess replied as she sat down at her dressing table and stared at herself in the mirror. A little Visine to get the redness out of her eyes.

Just a touch of makeup to make the puffiness around her eyes look less pronounced. Finally Jess brushed out her hair and stood up. She was in no shape to see anybody, but somehow she was going to have to face Andy.

She went to the door and opened it. Andy gave her a funny look. "You okay?"

Jess shrugged and turned away from the door. Andy followed her in and closed the door.

"Your mom said you wouldn't speak to anyone on the phone and you wouldn't come out of your room," Andy said. "What's wrong?"

Jess knew she couldn't tell him. If Andy found out she'd been with Reed, there was a chance he'd walk out on her. And right now she couldn't afford to let that happen.

She sat down on the bed. Andy sat down next to her. "I know that you know how to talk, Jess."

Jess took a deep breath and let it out slowly. "I . . . I don't know, Andy. It's just really hard for me right now."

"The whole thing with Gary?" Andy guessed.

Jess nodded even though that wasn't what it was about.

"I thought Reed had gotten you to look at it a different way," Andy said.

Jess just shrugged. She was afraid that if she uttered Reed's name she would burst into tears.

"So how was the party last night?" Andy asked, apparently deciding it was time to change the subject.

The next thing Jess knew, tears were welling up in her eyes and she couldn't stop them.

"Jeez, Jess, what's wrong?" Andy asked, sliding an arm around her shoulders.

Jess shook her head and sobbed. "Just hold me, Andy," she whispered.

Andy stayed with her until dinnertime. Jess couldn't believe how good and patient he was, and she hated herself for not telling him the truth. But she just couldn't.

"I really have to go, Jess," he said finally. "I've been away all week and my mother expects me home for dinner."

"God, I didn't even ask you about your trip," Jess gasped.

"It's okay," Andy assured her as he got up. "It was real quiet. I spent a lot of time looking at the clouds."

"Well, thanks for staying," Jess said. "You've been really great."

"So what are you going to do?" Andy asked.

The question caught Jess by surprise. "What am I going to do about what?"

"Well, about everything, I guess," Andy said. "I mean, starting with work tomorrow."

Jess hadn't even thought about that. How could she go back to being a lifeguard tomorrow? How could she look at Lisa and Reed without wanting to kill them? No, this was the end. She couldn't possibly go. She never wanted to be in the same room, on the same beach, or even in the same town with them again for as long as she lived.

"I don't know, Andy," she said. "I guess I'm going to have to think about all this some more."

Andy had to go. No sooner had he gone than Mrs. Sloat was at the bedroom door to tell her that Lisa had called again, and so had Reed. Jess said she'd call them back later, but she had no intention of doing it. It was still so hard to believe what they'd done. Jess took the tape back to the VCR and played it one more time just to make sure she hadn't made some kind of mistake. But as she watched the fuzzy gray images of Reed and Lisa kiss one more time, she knew there was no mistake.

Why did they keep calling? Was it to find out if she suspected anything?

Jess was taking the tape out of the VCR when her mother stepped into the den. "Dinner's on the table. I know you must be hungry. You haven't had a thing to eat all day."

The last thing Jess wanted to do was sit with her parents and eat. Besides, she had absolutely no appetite. But she also knew if she didn't eat, her mother would hover by her door all night fretting and worrying about her.

"I, uh, told Ellie I'd meet her for dinner in town," Jess said.

"Ellie?" Mrs. Sloat looked puzzled.

"She's the lifeguard I sit with," Jess explained.

"Well, don't be home too late," her mother said.

Jess said she wouldn't be. She went back to her room and got her wallet and then left the house. She had no idea where she was going.

As she started to walk down the sidewalk away from her house, a dozen possibilities ran through her head. Maybe she should go away for a while. Maybe she could go visit one of her relatives for a week, or the rest of the summer, or even the whole year! Or maybe she would go off and live by herself like a hermit. Out of reach of all these people who used her and lied and betrayed her.

Or maybe she'd just go to town and walk around. She got out to the main road and sat

down on the bench beside the bus stop, feeling
miserable and lonely and wishing she knew what
to do. She hardly noticed that a car had pulled
up to the curb in front of her.

"Hey, Jess."

Jess looked up. It was Billy in his jeep.

"Oh, hi, Billy."

"Waiting for the bus to town?" Billy asked.

"I guess." Jess shrugged.

"Want a ride?"

Jess stared at him. "What are you doing here?"

"I don't know," Billy said. "I was just driving
around. I mean, it's not like I have a lot to do
these days, you know?"

Jess knew. She felt the same way. Suddenly
she felt like she had no one to hang out with,
and no one to talk to.

"Are you headed into town?" she asked.

Billy stared down the road and then back at
her. "Tell you the truth, Jess, I don't know where
I'm headed."

Jess took a step toward the jeep and then
stopped. "This isn't a trick, is it?"

Billy stared at her. Jess half expected him to
get angry, but he just looked sad. "No, Jess, it's
not a trick. But if it worries you, you don't have
to come."

"Why would you take me?" she asked.

Billy shrugged. "Town sounds as good as any-place else."

It sounded to Jess like they were two peas in the same pod. Jess got into the jeep and Billy started to drive.

"So how was the party last night?" he asked.

The question sparked something in Jess's mind. "Did you leave that tape for me?"

"Huh?" Billy gave her a puzzled look.

"The tape of Reed and Lisa."

"Reed and Lisa?" Billy looked interested. "On the same tape?"

Jess nodded.

"What were they doing?"

"Don't ask," Jess said. He seemed innocent.

"Hey, you can't leave me hanging like that," Billy said.

"I'm sorry, Billy," Jess said. "I shouldn't have brought it up. Can we drop it?"

Billy looked disappointed, but then nodded. He didn't say another word to her the rest of the way into town. Finally they turned onto Main Street and he pulled up to the curb.

"Here you go," he said.

Jess looked around at the shops and restaurants and crowds of tourists. She quickly realized she had no desire to be there.

"Know what?" she said, turning to Billy. "I don't feel like going here anymore."

Billy just nodded. He didn't seem surprised. "Maybe I can drop you someplace else."

Jess shook her head. She actually couldn't think of anyplace she wanted to go. "Where were you going to go?" she asked.

"Me?" Billy chuckled and shook his head. "I told you, I wasn't going anywhere. I'm just burning gas."

Jess gazed across the seat at him. Unlike everyone else, Billy was making no demands on her. He appeared to have no expectations, either. He seemed completely prepared to drop her off and not see her again. Suddenly the idea of just driving around seemed attractive to her. The constant movement might help soothe her.

"You think I could go with you?" she asked.

Billy looked surprised. "You mean, just cruise around?"

Jess nodded. "But not around here. Let's drive somewhere where nobody knows us."

Billy turned the jeep around and headed back out of town on the narrow winding road that ran along the bluffs above the beach. It was another pretty sunset, and driving along with the wind in her hair, Jess felt a little better.

"I thought you had a curfew," Jess said.

Billy nodded. "I do, but it's the help's night off and my old man's out of town. I left the phone off the hook, so there's no way anyone will know I'm not there." He gestured toward the jeep's radio. "You want the radio?"

"Uh, sure," Jess said.

Soon they were cruising along, listening to music. Although she still felt terrible, Jess also felt comforted in a strange way. At least she was with someone who seemed to understand that she wanted to be left alone.

They drove for a while and then Billy pulled into a small dirt lot above a cliff overlooking the ocean. A sign at the end of the lot said that this was a scenic overlook, and Jess had to admit that the view of the waves and the water was nice. But she was nervous about stopping in the middle of nowhere with Billy. Had she been wrong to go with him? Was he going to try something?

Without a word, Billy got out of the jeep and walked to the edge of the cliff. He stood there for a while with his back to Jess, just staring down. Then he took off his tennis shoes. A moment later, without warning, he jumped.

"Billy!" Jess gasped. She couldn't believe it. She jumped out of the jeep and dashed to the edge of the cliff. Looking down, she saw Billy about fifteen feet below. So it wasn't a straight drop after all. Instead, the sandy face of the cliff sloped steeply down. Billy was standing in the face of the cliff with his feet buried halfway up his shins in a smooth, light-brown mixture of sand and dirt. As she watched, Billy crouched down and sprang forward, momentarily launching himself into the air and then landing in the sand farther down the cliff.

Jess took off her shoes and stepped to the edge of the cliff. It seemed like a steep drop and she felt scared. All the same, she took a deep breath and jumped. It was an amazing sensation — the closest she'd ever come to flying. And landing in the sand was painless. Just as Billy had done, Jess pulled her feet out of the sand and jumped again.

Below her, Billy reached the beach at the bottom of the cliff and looked back up at her. His face was expressionless and he nodded slightly. Then, without a word, he walked around to a ravine and climbed back up.

On her last jump, Jess landed at the base of the cliff where the beach began. She'd seen Billy walk off to the right and she followed him to the ravine. Billy had already climbed halfway back up to the top of the cliff. Jess started to follow.

They each jumped down the face of the cliff

four times and climbed back up. After the fifth time, instead of climbing back up, Billy walked across the beach to an old sun-bleached log and sat down. A few moments later Jess joined him. They were both gasping for breath.

"Do you do that a lot?" Jess asked.

"Just sometimes."

"It's fun," Jess said.

"It's different," Billy said, still breathing hard. "It's like a different sensation. When I jump and start falling through the air . . . for that second or two I feel totally free. I almost feel like I'm on a different planet."

"I know what you mean," Jess said. For the last few minutes, she'd actually *not* thought about Reed and Lisa for the first time all day.

It was starting to get dark. Sitting on the log, Jess stared at the waves and sand along this desolate strip of beach. She was glad Billy had brought her there, glad that he'd helped her see that there were things to do and people to be with besides Lisa and Reed. It still hurt to think about them, but at least there was life without them.

"So what do you want to do now?" Jess asked.

"I don't know, what do you want to do?" Billy said.

Jess didn't know what she wanted to do,

either. But she definitely knew what she *didn't* want to do. She didn't want to go back to Far Hampton and see any of those people she'd once called her friends.

On the other hand, it was growing darker and she was a little nervous about being alone on this desolate stretch of beach with Billy.

"Maybe we should get back in the car and ride some more," she said.

"Okay," Billy said.

It seemed as if they drove around in the dark for hours just listening to the radio. Neither of them said a thing, which Jess imagined was the way they both wanted it. It wasn't like they were going to become friends or anything. They were just two people who needed to be with someone who didn't make demands or remind them of how yucky things were.

Finally it was late and Jess asked Billy to drive her home. As Billy turned the jeep onto her street, Jess knew she'd succeeded in at least one goal. It was late enough now that she had a legitimate excuse for not calling anyone back.

Billy stopped the jeep outside her house, but for some strange reason Jess didn't get out right away. Instead, she looked across the seat at him.

"You were right about Reed," she said.

"About what?" Billy asked.

"What you said," Jess said.

Billy frowned in the dark as if he wasn't sure what she was talking about.

"About him wanting to have four girls by the end of the summer, remember?" Jess said.

"How come you believe me now and you didn't believe me a couple of days ago?"

"I just do," Jess said.

"Does this have something to do with that tape of Reed and Lisa?" Billy asked.

Jess nodded.

Billy shrugged. "You're lucky you didn't get involved with him again."

Jess nodded again quietly. If only Billy knew . . .

She got out and said good-bye. Billy gave her a terse nod and then drove away into the night. Jess stood on the curb and watched the jeep's taillights disappear into the dark. She wasn't sure what to make of Billy or the time she'd spent with him that evening, but she was glad he'd been there. It would have been hard to spend the time alone.

Jess turned and walked slowly up the slate path to her house. She knew she still faced a decision — what to do about lifeguarding? Earlier in the evening she had been convinced that this time she really was going to quit. But somehow being with Billy had changed her mind. She wouldn't give Lisa and Reed the satisfaction of seeing her quit. She would keep lifeguarding for Gary's sake. And try to find a life of her own.

NINE

Jess knew it wasn't going to be easy to go to work the next morning. She was almost certain that Lisa would want to drive by the bus stop and give her a ride. But Jess was wrong. Lisa wasn't waiting at the bus stop for her. Instead, she was waiting in the street outside Jess's house.

"Are you okay?" Lisa asked as Jess left her house.

"Like you really care," Jess said and walked right past her.

"Of course I care," Lisa said, following her. "I mean, what's going on? How come you didn't answer my calls yesterday?"

"I'm sorry, Lisa," Jess said. "I don't have anything to say to you."

"What are you talking about?" Lisa gasped.

"You know *exactly* what I'm talking about," Jess replied and kept walking.

"Jess, if I knew what you were talking about,

do you think I'd be asking?" Lisa said.

"Yes," Jess replied. "If you wanted to pretend nothing happened."

Lisa reached forward and grabbed Jess's arm to stop her. "Listen to me, Jess. I swear to God I don't know what you're talking about."

"Yes, you do," Jess said, pulling her arm out of Lisa's grasp.

"Okay, wait a minute," Lisa said. "Just humor me. Let's pretend I don't know. You tell me what you think is going on and I'll tell you if you're right."

Jess stared at her. "Why are you doing this?"

"Why?" Lisa said. "Because I really have no idea what you're talking about. That's why."

It was incredible, Jess thought. Lisa was putting on a great act. Jess almost would have believed her if it hadn't been for one thing.

"You're very convincing, Lisa," Jess said. "There's just one problem. I saw the tape."

"Tape?" Lisa looked at Jess as if she were crazy. "What tape?"

For the first time Jess realized that Lisa might not know about the tape. In fact, the more she thought about it, the more likely it was that Lisa had no idea a tape had been made. After all, what happened with Reed wasn't something she'd want everyone to know about.

"Someone made a tape of you," Jess said. "And I saw it. So don't bother denying it."

"A tape of me?" Lisa was acting completely bewildered. "What was I doing?"

Jess rolled her eyes. "Give me a break, Lisa. You know *exactly* what you were doing."

Lisa thought for a moment and then shook her head. "Listen, Jess, if you're so certain about this, would you please tell me? Because I still don't have a clue."

"I'm talking about Reed," Jess said.

"*Reed?*" Lisa scowled. "What about him?"

"*You* and Reed," Jess said.

"*Me* and Reed? What did we do?"

Jess stared at her for a moment, then shook her head and started walking toward the bus stop again. This time Lisa didn't follow.

"I don't know where you got a tape of me and Reed or what's on it," Lisa called behind her. "But Reed and I never did anything."

Jess took the bus to the beach. Despite her confrontation with Lisa, she still managed to get there a little early. She was just passing the lifeguard shack when Reed came running out.

"Jess?"

Jess just kept walking toward the West Wing chair and hoping Reed wouldn't follow her. He *had* to know why she was mad. She just hoped he had the guts not to play dumb the way Lisa had.

"Hey, wait a minute."

The next thing Jess knew, Reed was jogging across the sand toward her. "I called you yesterday. Didn't your mother tell you?"

Jess nodded and kept walking.

"What's going on, Jess?" Reed asked. "Why didn't you call back?"

Jess didn't want to go through the same scene with Reed that she'd just gone through with Lisa. It would be too upsetting to hear Reed lie. She turned and faced him.

"Reed, please," she said. "I know what happened and I don't want to talk about it. The best thing to do is just agree that it's over between us. Then you can go ahead and fulfill your goal for this summer. Oh, and by the way, have a good life."

She turned and started to walk away. But just as Lisa had earlier, Reed started to follow.

"Jess, I swear I don't have the slightest idea what you're talking about," he said. "What happened? What's my goal for this summer?"

Instead of answering, Jess just kept walking and praying Reed wouldn't press the point.

"Jess?" Reed called out behind her.

Jess stopped and turned once again. "It's over, Reed. That's the only thing that matters. I don't want to talk about it and I don't want to hear all your explanations and lies. We'll just pretend nothing ever happened and leave it at that."

Jess turned back toward the West Wing chair. She prayed Reed wouldn't follow her. She didn't want him to see the tears streaming out of her eyes.

Reed was already in the Main chair when Lisa got to work. She climbed up and joined him.

"Did you talk to Jess this morning?" Lisa asked.

Reed nodded and kept staring out at the ocean.

"Can I ask what she said?" Lisa asked.

"She doesn't want to see me anymore," Reed replied in a monotone.

"Did she happen to tell you why?" Lisa asked.

Reed shook his head. "I don't know, maybe I shouldn't be surprised. It seems like she changes faster than the weather."

"She told me she saw a tape of you and me," Lisa said.

Reed was so surprised he actually took his eyes off the patrons and turned and stared at her. "What?"

"A tape of you and me," Lisa said. "Don't ask me to explain because I can't."

"What are we doing on this tape?" Reed asked.

"I don't have a clue," Lisa said.

"Unbelievable," Reed muttered and stared back at the ocean.

Lisa took a long walk during lunch break. She was really depressed. It was terrible to be blamed for something you didn't do. And the fact that Jess was the one doing the blaming made it even more awful. Without Jess, Lisa had no girl friends in Far Hampton. No one to gossip with, no one to go browsing with in stores where they couldn't afford to buy anything. Jess appeared to be convinced that Lisa was somehow involved with Reed. That would probably dash Lisa's hopes of Andy seeing Jess and Reed get together again. Now Lisa would never be able to get Andy to pay attention to *her*.

Lisa found a spot in the dunes where no one could see her. She sat down and listened to the scratchy sound of the dune grass waving in the breeze. How could Jess have seen a tape of her and Reed together? What could they possibly have been doing? Carrying grocery bags?

"Lisa?"

Lisa looked up. She couldn't see him, but it sounded like Andy.

"Andy?" she said, surprised.

"Yeah, where are you?"

"Over here."

Andy came over the dunes and found her. "Hey, what's up?"

"How did you know I was here?" Lisa asked.

"I saw you walking toward the dunes," Andy explained. "I couldn't figure out where you were going so I decided I'd better check it out." He paused and studied her. "You okay?"

"No." Lisa stared down at the sand.

"Why?" Andy asked, crouching down next to her. "What's wrong?"

"You don't want to know," Lisa said. She also didn't want to tell him.

"Try me," Andy said, sitting down on the sand beside her.

Lisa gazed at him. He seemed sincere. It was nice to have his attention finally. The last thing she wanted to do was be unfriendly. So she told him about Jess and the story of the tape. When she finished, Andy looked upset.

"So . . . you and Reed are fooling around, huh?" he asked.

"No!" Lisa gasped. "*Me* and Reed, Andy? Are you serious?"

"Why not?" Andy asked. "You're really cute. You think Reed wouldn't notice that?"

Lisa was a bit shocked. Reed might not have noticed, but it seemed that Andy had. She couldn't help smiling a little. "I appreciate the compliment, Andy. But I don't think he did."

"You sure you're not fooling around with Reed?" Andy asked.

"I swear, Andy."

"Then I don't get it," Andy said. "I mean, Jess isn't crazy. If she says she saw a tape of you with Reed, then you have to believe she probably did."

"It's *not* possible, Andy," Lisa said, shaking her head. "I swear Reed and I have never done anything like that."

Andy thought for a moment. "Well, at least I understand one thing."

"What's that?" Lisa asked.

"Yesterday I went over to Jess's after I got back from my trip," Andy said. "She was totally bummed out, but she wouldn't tell me why."

"Now you know," Lisa said with a sigh.

Andy looked up at the sky. It was a breezy day and little white puff ball clouds were blowing past. He turned and looked back at Lisa.

"Just pretend for a second," he said. "Pretend she really did see a tape of you and Reed."

"But she couldn't have!" Lisa insisted.

"I know, I know," Andy said. "But pretend she did. Why would she be that upset?"

Lisa stared at him. "You mean, you don't know?"

"I know that just before I left to go to New Hampshire last week Jess pretty much swore to me she wouldn't get involved with him again," Andy said.

Lisa bit her lip. She picked up a handful of sand and let it seep down through her fingers.

"Did something change while I was gone?" Andy asked.

Lisa nodded.

"Want to tell me?" Andy asked.

"They were together all week," she said. "The night of the party they left together."

"You know where they went?" Andy asked.

Lisa shook her head. "All I know is that when I called Jess's house at noon the next day, her mother said she was still asleep."

Andy looked down at the sand. He had to admit he wasn't surprised. He'd left Jess for a week and she went straight back to Reed. It seemed like nothing he did counted. Nothing he said mattered. Andy shook his head slowly.

"I don't know why I even bother," he muttered.

"Bother with what?" Lisa asked.

"Bother to care about Jess," Andy said. "Bother to try and stop her from getting into a situation where she's going to get really hurt. I mean, I warned her that Reed would hurt her."

"I guess you were right," Lisa said. "Only he didn't do it with me. . . ."

Andy looked up. "Huh?"

Lisa bit her lip. "If I tell you, will you swear you won't tell a soul?"

Andy nodded.

"Before the party, Reed and I got to the boat early to get ready," Lisa said. "I don't know how it happened, but Paula wound up in the water off the dock."

Andy frowned. "What do you mean, she wound up in the water?"

"She had some story about jumping off a boat or something," Lisa said. "Anyway, she was soaking wet and she said she couldn't go home, so I left Reed and her on the boat and went to get her some dry clothes. Well, when I got back, Reed and Paula were together in the bedroom."

Andy's eyes went wide. "You serious?"

"I walked in by accident," Lisa said. "They

were just hugging, but Paula didn't have much on."

Andy shook his head. "You know, I almost feel like Jess deserves it. I mean, I did everything I could to keep her away from Reed and she went back to him the second I left for New Hampshire. It's hopeless. Totally hopeless. I've had it."

Lisa stared at Andy, feeling bad for him. His words should have been music to her ears, but instead she couldn't help feeling sorry. How could she not sympathize with someone who'd finally realized that the girl he'd liked for so long would never be his?

The next thing she knew, she slid her arm around his shoulders.

"Andy?" she whispered.

Andy looked up at her. "Yeah?"

"I'm really, really sorry," Lisa whispered.

Andy gazed back into Lisa's big brown eyes. It was funny how she was always around, but he'd never really paid attention to her before. Not *serious* attention, anyway. He'd always been so preoccupied with Jess. And if he'd ever thought about Lisa, it was always in comparison to Jess. But it was pretty obvious now that it was time to forget about Jess. And if he just looked at Lisa for what she was, and not as a comparison, she was really a nice kid. And sensitive. And *very* cute.

"I think maybe I've made a big mistake," Andy said softly, moving his face closer to hers.

"How?" Lisa whispered. She felt a tremor inside as he came closer. Her heart started to beat hard. Could this really be happening?

"Well, I think maybe I've been looking for something that's been here all along," Andy whispered.

A second later, he kissed her.

Lying on a sand dune twenty feet away, Billy kept his small video camera trained on Andy and Lisa. It was just by accident that he'd come across them while picking up litter. He was glad to get those two kissing on tape. Things were working out very nicely, indeed.

All afternoon, Reed's feelings alternated between bewilderment and anger. He was bewildered that Jess had changed yet again. And angry that she had the nerve to treat him the way she did. Who did she think she was, anyway?

But every time Reed asked himself that question, he got the same answer. She was the girl he was crazy about. And he liked her too much to stay angry for long. So the best thing he could do was find out what was going on.

Reed waited until the end of the day before he tried to speak to Jess again. Now that Jess was angry with Lisa, Reed knew she wouldn't get a ride home with her. And that meant she'd have to take the bus. But at the end of the day Jess seemed to have disappeared. She wasn't on the beach or around the lifeguard shack. When Reed got in his jeep and drove up to the bus stop on the beach road, he found that it was empty.

Reed sat in his car on the side of the road and looked up and down the thin strip of asphalt. It didn't make sense. Jess couldn't have gotten a ride with anyone else, and she couldn't have disappeared. Unless . . .

Reed quickly turned the jeep around and drove down the beach road. The next closest bus stop was about half a mile away, in an area of beach houses. As Reed got closer, he could see the beach bus coming in the opposite direction. Just as Reed had suspected, Jess got on. Reed quickly pulled his jeep to the side of the road and sprinted across the street to the bus stop. The bus driver was just closing the doors when Reed banged on them with his fist. The doors opened and Reed climbed on.

Jess thought she'd have a heart attack when Reed jumped on the bus. Now he was walking down the aisle toward her. The bus was practically empty.

"Excuse me," he said, gesturing to the empty seat next to her. "Is this seat taken?"

Jess turned and stared out the window. She simply couldn't believe he'd found her. Meanwhile, Reed sat down.

"So you walked down the beach to a bus stop where you thought no one would find you," Reed said. "Gee, Jess, it must be tough, having to avoid everyone."

Jess continued to stare out the window.

"Anyway," Reed said. "Lisa told me about this tape you say you saw. It sounds really interesting. I was wondering if maybe I could come back to your house and see it. Since I'm starring in it."

Jess turned and glared at him. "Don't you have anything better to do?"

"You know, I'd really appreciate it if you'd stop treating me like dirt," Reed said, clenching his teeth.

"You don't think you deserve it?" Jess asked.

"No."

"Look," Jess said. "Why don't you just get off the bus and go find one more girl so that you can achieve your goal for the summer. Or maybe you need to find more than one. After all, I don't know what you did with Paula and the tape with Lisa isn't that revealing."

Reed stared at her for a few moments without replying. "This is getting more interesting all the time. I'd really like to know more about my goal for the summer."

"Right." Jess scoffed at his words. "Like you don't know."

"Well, I can see there's no point in trying to tell *you* that," Reed said. "Since you seem to know more about what I know than I do."

Jess just shook her head and stared out the window again.

"You know," Reed said. "I think the thing that really kills me is that I've been found guilty without a trial. I mean, usually you're innocent until proven guilty. Except here I don't even get a chance to prove that I'm innocent."

"The evidence against you is pretty strong," Jess replied.

"Oh, really?" Reed said. "You know, we

studied the judicial system in school last year. Lawyers have something called discovery. That means that in a court case one side has to show all its evidence to the other side."

"Well, this isn't a court case," Jess replied.

"That's for sure," Reed said.

The bus stopped and a crowd of kids wearing bathing suits and carrying towels and boogie boards got on.

"Hey, look, it's the lifeguards!" one of them shouted. The next thing Reed and Jess knew, the kids were jamming into the seats around them.

"I didn't think you guys had to take the bus," said a tall skinny kid with curly black hair.

"Yeah," said a chubby kid with a blond crew-cut. "I always see you cruising around in that jeep."

Reed smiled. "Sometimes even lifeguards travel by public transportation."

"Hey, how do you get to be a lifeguard anyway?" another kid asked.

Reed spent the rest of the ride answering questions while Jess sat silently. Finally they got to her street. The bus pulled over and Jess got up.

"Excuse me, guys," Reed said to the kids. "This is our stop." Reed got up and followed

Jess off the bus. A moment later the bus pulled away and left them standing by the side of the road in a cloud of exhaust fumes.

"Good-bye, Reed," Jess said and started across the street.

"Wait a minute, Jess," Reed said, following her. "I wasn't finished."

"As far as I'm concerned you were," Jess said, reaching the other side of the road. She quickly started walking down the street toward her house.

"You know, I really can't *believe* you," Reed said. "How can you act like this after all we've been through?"

Jess spun on her heels and glared at him. "After what *we've* been through? Tell me, Reed, what have *you* been through, other than at least three girls this summer?"

Reed set his jaw. "*Your* brother didn't betray you, Jess. Mine did. You weren't arrested. And no one gave you a private monopoly on feeling bad about Gary. I was there, too. Now, I still don't know why you're so mad at me *this time*, but I've just about had it with you constantly accusing me of things I didn't do. How about listening to *me* for once?"

"Listen to you?" Jess replied icily. "Why? So you can tell me how we're going to sail together all fall and spring? So we can cross the Atlantic together next summer?" Jess shook her head angrily. "God, I can't believe I fell for that line. What in the world was I thinking?"

"I was serious," Reed said.

"Oh, really?" Jess glared at him. "Then you better trade in *Simplicity* and get a bigger sailboat, because I'm sure all the other girls you've used that line on think they're going, too."

Once again Jess spun around and stormed off. Only this time, Reed didn't follow.

Billy had just enough time to drop off the tape at Paula's and get back home before his curfew. He knew he was taking a risk by getting Paula to leave the tape at Jess's house later, but there was no way he could have done it himself tonight. He wouldn't tell Paula what was on the tape, and warned her not to watch it. All she had to do was wait until all the lights were off at Jess's house and leave it outside the front door.

Billy hadn't been home very long when he heard the door slam downstairs. Then he heard footsteps bang up the stairs. A second later another door slammed.

Billy smiled. Reed must have come home, and it sounded like he was seriously ticked off.

He waited a little while to give his brother some time to cool down. Billy and Reed hadn't had much to say to each other since Reed had discovered Billy stole the radar and hid it on *Simplicity*. Billy still didn't understand Reed's reaction to that incident. It seemed to Billy that if he had been in Reed's position and learned that his brother had set him up, got him in trouble with the police, and tried to put the moves on his girlfriend, he probably would've beaten the guy into a bloody pulp with a baseball bat.

But Reed's attitude was different. He was more "philosophical" about these things. His attitude was to forgive and forget. And if Reed couldn't completely forget what Billy had done, then he just wouldn't talk to him for a while.

Billy got up and left his room and went down the hall. He knocked on Reed's door.

"Who is it?" Reed asked from inside.

"Billy."

There was a long pause. Then Reed said, "Come in."

Billy opened the door and stepped in. It had been a long time since he'd been in his brother's room. Of course, being a perfect person, Reed kept his room in perfect condition. There were posters of sailboats on the walls and model sailboats on the shelves. The bookcases were filled with books and rows of soccer, tennis, and basketball trophies.

Reed was sitting at his desk. He looked upset. "What's up now, Billy?"

Billy leaned in the doorway. "Not much. I was just wondering what was going on with the crew. I never get to talk to anyone anymore."

"Everything's fine," Reed said.

"Anyone make any exciting rescues lately?" Billy asked.

Reed shook his head.

"Ever see any of Gary Pilot's friends?" Billy asked.

"Yeah, they come around once in a while," Reed said.

Billy waited in the doorway quietly for a few moments before asking the next question. "You still seeing Jess?"

Reed just stared back at him for the longest time. Then he said, "No."

Jess sat alone in her room again that night. But unlike the previous night, the phone didn't ring. Of course, Jess didn't expect to hear from Lisa or Reed, but she was surprised that Andy didn't call. She hadn't had a chance to speak to him all day and normally he would have called by now to see how the day had gone. When Andy still hadn't called by ten o'clock, Jess decided to call him.

"Hello?" Mrs. Moncure answered.

"Hi, it's Jess. Is Andy home?"

"Uh, no, Jess," Andy's mother said.

"Oh, uh, did he say where he was going?" Jess asked.

"No," Mrs. Moncure said. "He didn't come home after work today. I really don't know where he is. But I'll tell him you called."

"Thanks." Jess hung up, feeling uncomfortable. Where would Andy be at that hour? Who would he have gone out with without automatically asking Jess if she wanted to come, too?

Jess sat down on her bed and turned on the TV, but nothing caught her interest. She kept thinking about Reed and Andy. Of course, Andy had been right about Reed all along and she'd simply been too blind to see it. What she could see now was how much Andy must have cared to keep trying to protect her like that. Jess felt like a fool. She'd fallen for the oldest cliché in the book — the grass was always greener on the other side. She should have been happy with Andy. She shouldn't have asked for more.

Jess tried to watch the TV, but her eyes kept going to the radio alarm clock beside the bed. It was now ten-thirty. Where could Andy possibly be? And with whom? Jess recalled Mrs. Moncure saying that Andy hadn't come home after work. That probably meant that whoever he was with was someone who drove.

A car door slammed out front. *It must have been Andy!* Jess hopped off her bed and ran through the house to the front door. But as soon as she got to the front door she was disappointed. It was just her father. He'd gotten a ride home from one of the men on the police force and was now leaning in the car window, chatting with him.

Suddenly Jess had an idea and went outside. "Uh, Dad?"

Chief Sloat looked up. "Hey, Jess what's up?"

"Do you think I could get a lift over to Andy's apartment?" Jess asked.

Her father looked surprised. "It's kind of late, isn't it?"

"I'll probably just be a second," Jess said. "I'm sure Andy will give me a ride home."

"Well, if it's okay with Don," Chief Sloat said. Don Pfeffer was one of the officers on the police force. Jess leaned down and waved at him through the window.

"Hi, Officer Pfeffer," she said.

"Hi, Jess," the police officer waved back and pushed the door open. "Sure, I'll give you a ride. It's no problem."

Jess smiled and got in his car. There were certain advantages to being the daughter of the chief of police.

A few minutes later, Officer Pfeffer dropped Jess off in front of Andy's apartment above the hardware store in town. It was almost eleven o'clock and most of the shops were closed up. Only a few restaurants remained open. Jess was certain Andy would be home by now.

She was just about to go up the stairs to Andy's apartment when she heard a familiar sound coming down the street. Jess would have recognized it anywhere. It was the sound of Lisa's car. She turned to watch as the VW came to a stop at the curb near a streetlight. Inside, both Andy and Lisa looked surprised to see her.

Jess waited for Andy to get out. In the car Andy said something to Lisa that Jess couldn't hear. Lisa nodded. Andy got out and Lisa quickly drove away.

"Jess," Andy said, walking across the sidewalk toward her. "What are *you* doing here?"

"I just wanted to see you," Jess said. "What were you doing with Lisa?"

Andy shrugged. "Uh, she told me about the tape. She was real upset about it, Jess. She just needed to talk."

"I didn't know you two had gotten so friendly," Jess said.

"Well, I guess she feels like she doesn't have anyone else she can talk to," Andy said.

"She must have had a lot to say," Jess said. "I called before and your mom said you've been out since after work."

"Well, yeah," Andy said. He scuffed his tennis shoe against the curb and looked up at her. "So, uh, what's up?"

Jess came close and put her hands on his shoulders. "Are you still my best friend, Andy?"

"Well, uh, sure I am, Jess," Andy said.

"Positive?" Jess asked.

Andy scowled. "What's going on?"

"Well, it may sound silly, but I just wanted to know that you were still there and you still cared," Jess said. "I mean, after everything that's happened, I feel like you're the only person left I can still trust."

Andy reached up and took her hands off his shoulders, but he held onto them.

"It's kind of hard to believe that you came all the way here at eleven o'clock at night just to tell me that," he said.

"Do you want me to go?" Jess asked, surprised.

"No," Andy said.

Suddenly Jess felt a little awkward standing there on the sidewalk with him. Andy hadn't exactly greeted her with open arms, nor did he seem to want to invite her in.

"So, uh, what do you want to do now?" Andy asked.

Jess shrugged. "I don't know." She smiled sheepishly. "Probably go home. Can you give me a ride?"

Andy seemed to nod almost too quickly. "Wait here. I'll get the keys to the car."

Jess waited while Andy went inside. He was definitely acting strangely. She wondered if it had anything to do with Lisa. Certainly his new friendship with her couldn't be too serious. Reed had taken care of *that*.

Andy came back out and they got into his mother's old Buick.

"So how was your day?" he asked as they started back toward Jess's house. Jess looked at him in amazement.

"How was my day?" she repeated. "Fairly bizarre considering what I found out about Reed and Lisa. How was your day?"

Andy shrugged. "Okay, I guess."

"Did Lisa say anything about Reed?" Jess asked.

Andy shook his head. "I don't know what's on that tape, Jess. But I still find it hard to believe."

"Everyone keeps telling me that," Jess said. "I mean, do they really think I'd make such a thing up?"

"Well, no," Andy said. "But the idea that it's on tape . . . I mean, you don't think there's a chance that you're mistaken?"

"Believe me, Andy, if you saw the tape you'd know it was no mistake."

Andy snapped his fingers. "That's it, Jess. Let me see the tape!"

"No," Jess said, crossing her arms resolutely.

"Why not?"

"Because I can't believe you don't trust me," Jess said, feeling hurt. "I thought we were friends, Andy. I thought we were best friends."

"We are . . ." Andy began.

"Well, then I think it's about time you believed me," Jess said.

"It's not that I don't believe you, Jess," Andy said. "It's just that anyone can make a mistake."

But Jess didn't agree. "Believe me, Andy, I didn't."

They got to Jess's house. For a few moments

Andy and Jess sat in the car without saying anything. Jess could sense that something wasn't right. But she couldn't imagine what it was.

"Well, thanks for the ride," Jess said and started to get out of the car.

"Uh, Jess?" Andy said.

Jess turned back to him. "Yes?"

"For the last time, I'd really really like to see that tape. How about it?"

Jess thought about it for a moment, but then shook her head. "You have to believe me, Andy. If you're really my friend, you will."

"It's just so hard for me to believe that Reed and Lisa would be together," Andy said.

"Believe it," Jess said.

Andy started to say something more, but then shook his head.

"What were you going to say?" Jess asked.

"Uh, it was nothing."

"Okay, Andy, see you tomorrow." Jess closed the door and Andy pulled away. For a moment, Jess stood at the curb and watched. It seemed to her that suddenly everyone was acting very strange. She turned and started up the walk toward her house. As she reached the screen door, she noticed that a Manila envelope was propped up against it. Jess bent down and picked it up.

Inside she could feel something hard and rectangular.

It had to be another videocassette!

Her house was dark and quiet. Jess walked into the den and slid the cassette into the VCR. She flicked on the TV and stepped back and watched. Once again she saw black-and-white static, but this time it gave way to a bright, sunny day at the beach. The picture was much clearer and sharper than the one of Reed and Lisa. Now the scene changed to dunes covered with dune grass. The picture went out of focus and then refocused on a girl and a guy sitting close together with their backs to the camera. They were alone and the girl had her arm around the guy's shoulder. Suddenly they turned to face each other.

Jess gasped. It was Lisa and Andy!

A moment later Jess watched in total amazement as the two kissed.

Billy was in the middle of watching the original *Friday the 13th* on his TV when the phone rang. It was almost midnight.

"Hello?"

"Hi." It was Paula.

"You drop the tape off?" Billy asked.

"Yes."

"Anyone see you?"

"No."

"Good," Billy said. He wished he could be there when Jess popped *that* tape into her VCR.

"I'd really like to know what's going on," Paula said.

"Oh, yeah?" Billy chuckled. "I'll tell you what's going on. This would be a really good time for you to start hanging out with Reed again. I think my brother could use a friend."

TEN

Jess got very little sleep that night. It was just too incredible. First Reed and Lisa. Now Lisa and Andy. Jess wouldn't have believed any of it if she hadn't seen it with her own eyes. But now Jess understood why Andy had acted the way he had that night. *He was feeling guilty!*

And no wonder he was so interested in seeing the tape. If he liked Lisa, of course he'd want to make sure she wasn't fooling around with Reed. Well, if he didn't want to believe Jess, that was his problem.

Jess got to work late the next morning. It was just as well. At least this way Reed, Andy, and Lisa would already be in their chairs and she wouldn't have to face any of them. Jess walked out to the West Wing chair and climbed up. Ellie was already sitting there. She just nodded at Jess and turned back to scan the beach. Sometimes Jess wished she could talk to Ellie, but Ellie was the quiet type and older and had her own circle of friends.

It was a cool, overcast day and the beach was practically empty. Jess stared at the gray waves and the gray sky, feeling terribly alone. During the night she'd once again begun to wonder just who was leaving those videotapes for her. She no longer suspected Andy, and there was no reason why Paula would want her to see a tape of Andy and Lisa. That still left Billy, but what did *he* have to gain by leaving the tapes? The other possibility was that the tapes were being left by someone else altogether, but in a way it didn't matter. Whatever that person's motives were didn't change what was on the tapes themselves. The truth was unshakable: The three people Jess was closest to had all betrayed her.

Of all of them, Jess was angriest at Reed. It was easier to understand why Andy had turned to Lisa. After all, Jess had run hot and cold with him so many times and even now she wasn't certain if she really wanted him for a boyfriend or just a close friend.

And Lisa? Well, Jess was stung by what she'd done with Reed, but Reed had probably fed her the same lines he'd fed Jess. In fact, Jess was certain he must have. After all, Lisa wasn't the type of girl to get involved with a guy so quickly.

Not unless that guy had filled her head with a
lot of false promises and assurances. And as far
as Lisa going after Andy, Jess couldn't blame her
for that at all. Lisa had liked Andy for a long
time.

But Reed . . . There was no way Jess could
forgive him. He'd lied to her and used her. He'd
turned out to be everything Andy had said he
was. A smooth, good-looking snake.

For most of the morning, Reed and Lisa sat
silently in the Main chair. The beach was practically empty, except for some kids throwing a
football and an older guy with a metal detector
looking for lost change and jewelry. Reed sat
hunched forward, his elbows on his knees, staring pensively at the waves. Lisa knew he wasn't
watching swimmers.

"Did you talk to Jess?" she asked.

Reed nodded.

"I guess it didn't go so well," Lisa said.

Reed shook his head.

They sat and listened to the crashing of the
waves and the squawks of the sea gulls. Lisa
assumed Reed didn't feel like talking, so she was
surprised when he straightened up and turned to
her.

"I swear I'll never understand this," he said.

"She insists she has a tape of you and me together. She won't tell me what we were supposedly doing, but she hints that it's pretty bad. And she won't let me see it."

"I know," Lisa said with a sigh. "It's really strange."

"I realize Jess and I got off to a bad start," Reed said. "I mean, with what Billy did to me, and then Gary drowning. . . . But I thought we could get past those things, I really did. Now there's this. It really makes me wonder if it's worth it."

"It must be really frustrating," Lisa said.

"Well, I guess it just makes me question everything," Reed said. "Like, were Jess and I ever really meant to be together? I mean, are there basic differences that we'll just never be able to get past?"

"Like what?" Lisa asked.

Reed shrugged. Before he could continue, the phone attached to the lifeguard chair rang and Reed answered it. "Yeah, okay, I'll be right there."

"Hank?" Lisa guessed as he hung up.

"Yes," Reed said. "He's going to tell me that because of the weather he wants to trim down to a skeleton crew for the rest of the day."

*   *   *

Reed climbed down out of the chair and walked back up the beach. He looked to his left, down at the West Wing chair where Jess was sitting with Ellie. Reed shook his head sadly. He just didn't get it.

He stepped up on the porch of the lifeguard shack and knocked on the door.

"Come in," Hank yelled from inside.

Reed pushed open the door. Hank was seated in one of the old chairs listening to the marine weather forecast on the radio.

"What's up?" Reed asked.

"Forecast is for increasing cloudiness followed by drizzle and rain," the lifeguard captain said. "I thought we'd trim down to a skeleton crew."

"Senior guards stay, rookies get off?" Reed asked.

"It won't make much difference," Hank said. "I'll let each chair decide for themselves."

Reed nodded and headed back out. As he pushed open the door and went out onto the porch, he almost knocked over Paula, wearing a white sweatsuit.

"Jeez, Paula, I'm sorry," Reed apologized.

"Oh, it's okay," Paula said, regaining her balance.

"What are you doing here?" Reed asked.

"I was just looking for you," Paula said. "I knew it wouldn't be busy today and I thought maybe I could take you to lunch."

Reed didn't answer right away. He knew there was no such thing as a free lunch. Paula wanted something from him. Most likely she wanted to talk about getting back together. Once again Reed stared down at the West Wing chair where Jess was sitting. What were his options for the rest of the day? He could let Lisa go home and then he could spend the day sitting alone in the drizzling rain. Or he could go home and spend another lonely afternoon working on *Simplicity*. He turned back to Paula.

"When did you want to go?" he asked.

"Well, it's lunchtime now," Paula said.

"Okay," Reed said. "Just let me go tell Lisa."

Reed jogged down the beach to the Main chair. To his surprise, Lisa insisted that he take as long as he wanted. She knew he was the one who usually got stuck in the chair in bad weather. Reed thanked her.

Down the beach at the West Wing chair, the telephone rang and Jess watched Ellie answer it. She gathered Ellie was talking to Hank. After a moment, Ellie hung up.

"That was Hank," she said. "He says it may start to rain soon and he wants us to trim down to a skeleton crew. He said it's up to us to decide who stays."

Jess didn't particularly care. She didn't relish the idea of sitting in the chair alone in the rain, but she didn't have anything better to do at the moment.

"I'll stay if you want," she said.

"Would you?" Ellie replied. "I'd really appreciate it. I've got a mountain of dirty laundry at home and I've been waiting for a rainy day to do it."

Jess watched Ellie climb down from the chair and start to jog toward the lifeguard shack. She noticed that Reed had left the Main chair and was also walking back toward the shack. Now a girl wearing white joined him and they started walking toward the parking lot. Was she number four in Reed's quest to make his summer goal? Jess picked up the chair's binoculars and looked through them. Now she could see that the girl in white was Paula. That was strange. Jess would have thought Reed had already succeeded with her. But why should she care what Reed did anymore? Jess put the binoculars back down and stared out at the waves.

★　　★　　★

They took Paula's car and drove into town. Reed expected that she'd want to take him to one of the fancy bistros that now dotted Main Street. So he was surprised when she stopped at a small storefront sandwich shop called My Hero. A few minutes later she came back out with a brown paper bag and put it on the car seat between them. The tangy aromas of Italian spices wafted out of the bag as Paula started to drive again.

"Where are we going?" Reed asked.

"You'll see," Paula replied.

"You're just full of surprises today, aren't you?" Reed said.

Paula smiled at him, but didn't reply.

Soon Reed recognized the road that led to the harbor. A few moments later they parked on the side of the road on a hill overlooking Far Hampton harbor. It had started to drizzle, and thousands of tiny drops of water dotted the windshield of the car. Low clouds and patches of white fog drifted over the harbor and in and out of the boats moored there.

"Pretty, isn't it?" Paula asked as she pulled a liter bottle of Coke out of the bag on the front seat.

Reed nodded. "It is, Paula, but I don't get this."

"Get what?" Paula asked.

"Get us sitting here about to eat lunch in your car," Reed said. "I mean, no offense or anything, but this isn't your style, Paula."

"Maybe I've decided to change my style," Paula said. She took two paper cups out of the bag and poured them each some Coke.

"You've come to appreciate the joy of eating in your car?" Reed asked wryly.

"Maybe I'm just tired of everyone thinking I'm this rich, stuck-up snob who only likes to eat in expensive restaurants." Paula said. She held up her paper cup of Coke. "Cheers."

Reed tapped his cup against hers and laughed.

"What's so funny?" Paula asked with a puzzled grin.

"You can take the girl out of the restaurant, but you can't take the restaurant out of the girl," Reed said.

"What are you talking about?" Paula asked.

"I'm talking about toasting with paper cups of Coke," Reed said.

"I was just kidding," Paula said.

"Oh, sure," Reed replied with a smile.

Next, Paula reached into the grocery bag and pulled out a large bag of thick Hawaiian-style potato chips.

"Ahh, excellent," Reed said, tearing open the

bag and taking out a handful of chips. "What's next?"

Paula looked into the grocery bag, but started to frown.

"What's wrong?" Reed asked.

"Uh, nothing," Paula replied and slowly reached in and took out an Italian hero. The wax paper it had been wrapped in was now soaked through with oil and vinegar, and the paper itself had started to unfold. Trying to use only the tips of her fingers, Paula gingerly lifted the hero out of the bag. Drops of oil and vinegar had started dripping out of the wax paper onto the front seat.

"Help me," Paula cried. "It's leaking!"

Reed couldn't help laughing.

"What's so funny?" Paula gasped.

"You are," Reed said. He took the sandwich from her and placed it on top of the dashboard.

Paula's jaw fell open. "Reed! How could you?"

"How could I what?" Reed asked as he started to unfold the wax paper.

"You're getting oil and vinegar all over the dashboard," Paula said.

Reed lifted half the sandwich out of the paper and took a bite out of it. As he did, a few stringy lengths of shredded lettuce slid out and fell on the floor of the car.

Paula just stared at him in horror.

"Hey," Reed said with a chuckle. "Haven't you ever eaten in a car before?"

"You want to know the truth?" Paula asked. "The answer is never in my life. I wasn't allowed to eat in cars growing up. My father used to say that if you wanted to go out, you took the car. And if you wanted to eat out, you went to a restaurant."

"Well, this is what eating heros in cars is all about, Paula," Reed said. "I thought you said you were changing your style."

"I am," Paula said. "I just didn't anticipate that it meant having to have my car cleaned as well."

"You don't have to get your car cleaned," Reed explained. "You just get some paper towels and wipe it up."

"But it'll still be greasy," Paula said.

"Okay, then you use some Fantastik," Reed said.

Paula sighed. She very carefully lifted her hero out of the bag and then looked around for a place to put it. It seemed to Reed that she couldn't bear the thought of putting it on top of the dashboard.

"Here's another trick," Reed said. He took the brown paper grocery bag and folded it flat and then slid it onto Paula's lap. "Now you don't have to put it on the dashboard."

Paula put the hero down on the paper and started to unfold the greasy wax paper. For a few moments she just stared at the hero. Shreds of lettuce, edges of meat and cheese, and slices of tomatoes were sticking out everywhere.

"What's wrong now?" Reed asked.

"I'm terrified that if I try to pick it up, everything's going to slide right out and onto my lap," Paula confessed.

"You have to hold it properly," Reed instructed her. "Now watch. You use both hands, always applying pressure to the edges of the sandwich in order to prevent everything from spilling out."

Paula carefully tried to pick up the sandwich, pressing down on the edges. She almost got it to her mouth, when suddenly all the meat and cheese and tomatoes squirted out the bottom and landed with a *Plop!* on the folded grocery bag.

Paula stared down at the mess with wide eyes.

"Too much pressure," Reed said.

"What?" Paula looked up and scowled at him.

Reed held up his half-eaten sandwich. "You applied too much pressure to the edges. It pushed everything out the back."

"I see." Paula pushed open the car door,

picked up the flattened grocery bag and carried it like a tray to a roadside garbage can. She dropped the whole thing into the can and then returned to the car.

"It takes practice," Reed said, offering her the untouched half of his hero. "Want to try again?"

Paula shook her head. "Don't come near me with that. I've handled enough greasy sandwiches for one day."

"As you wish," Reed said and put the half of the sandwich back on the dashboard.

For a while they sat in the car without speaking. Reed finished his sandwich and washed it down with the rest of his Coke. Suddenly he noticed that tears were running down Paula's cheeks.

"Hey," he said. "What's wrong?"

"I hope you're happy," Paula sniffed.

"Why would I be happy?" Reed asked, handing her a clean napkin.

"Because you've proven that I can't be like all the other people around here who know how to eat heros in their cars," Paula said miserably as she dabbed her eyes with the napkin.

"Now wait a minute," Reed said. "Eating heros in the car was your idea, not mine. And I wasn't trying to prove anything."

"Oh, yes you were," Paula insisted. "You

think it's so great that you can be just like these people here in Far Hampton. Regular people. The salt of the earth.''

"I don't try to be like them," Reed said. "I just try to be me.''

"Then tell me this," Paula said. "Why are you a lifeguard while everyone else you know spends the summer sailing or traveling? Why do you insist on hanging out at the public beach when everyone else belongs to private clubs? Why do you date a local girl when everyone else dates their own kind?''

"Their own kind?" Reed echoed with a shocked look on his face.

"You know what I mean," Paula said. "People they go to school with.''

"This is the way I am, Paula," Reed said. "I don't see why I have to be defensive about it.''

"I'm not trying to make you defensive," Paula said. "This isn't an attack. I'm just trying to understand.''

"Understand why I don't feel the need to act like a preppy snob?" Reed asked with a smile.

"Let me ask you this," Paula said. "Do you think Hank and Lisa and the others really accept you as one of them?''

"Yes.''

Paula shook her head and sighed. "Reed, I

know that you really mean well. I know you think a lot of the people you grew up with are stuck-up snobs and you don't like to consider yourself one of them. But the truth is your father is one of the richest men in the country and you go to one of the most exclusive prep schools in the East. You can't pretend you don't. I mean, if you really like slumming around with these people, then fine. But don't try to pretend you're one of them."

Reed had been all ready to argue with her, but something stopped him. Was Paula right? Was he different from the other residents of Far Hampton? Jess's behavior, for instance, made no sense to him. Was the explanation simply that they were different?

Paula glanced across the seat at him. "Why aren't you arguing with me?"

Reed shrugged. "I don't know, Paula. I mean, deep in my heart I think you're wrong. But some things have happened lately that make me wonder. It's just . . . I don't know. It's hard for me to believe that we could be so different from other people just because of money."

"I'm not saying it's good or right or justifiable," Paula said. "I just don't think you can pretend it's not there. I mean, it's like me trying to eat a hero in my car. It's just not natural."

"But you could learn," Reed said.

"Yes, but I'd still be pretending," Paula said. "There'd always be this little voice in my head saying, *'If you want to go out, take the car, but if you want to eat out, go to a restaurant.'* "

Reed gathered up the wax paper from his sandwich and got out of the car to throw it out. The drizzle was just a fine mist, and after he threw his garbage in the can, he gazed out over Far Hampton harbor at the boats, the docks, the old lighthouse, and the small fish-processing factory where the commercial fishermen brought their catch.

He'd always liked Far Hampton. He'd always felt more comfortable there than in his father's Park Avenue apartment in the city or at St. Peter's. But maybe Paula was right. Because of who his father was and the way he'd been brought up, maybe he was different. And maybe that was why he couldn't understand Jess at all.

"Reed?"

Reed turned around and found Paula standing behind him. Her arms were crossed tightly in front of her and the tiny droplets of drizzle were catching in her hair.

"What are you doing out here, Paula?" Reed asked.

Paula stepped closer to him. "I . . . I just

wanted to be with you," she said in a voice that was hardly more than a whisper.

"Even in the rain?" Reed asked.

Paula nodded and stepped even closer. Now she was standing right next to him.

For a few moments they stood side by side, gazing down at the harbor as the drizzle collected on their hair and faces. Reed wondered if she was right. Maybe he was best off sticking with people like himself. At least with them he knew what to expect.

"Come on, Paula," he said, sliding his arm around her shoulder and guiding her back to the car. "We'd better get out of the rain."

It had started to drizzle harder. Jess climbed down from her chair and got some rain gear out of the box beneath it. She put it on and climbed back up. It was hard to believe, but the town's policy was that the beach was open every day regardless of the weather. And that meant that a lifeguard had to be on the beach, even in a hurricane. After all, you never knew when some crazy kid like Gary Pilot might want to come out and try boogie boarding in a storm.

But today there were no crazy boogie boarders in the waves. On her part of the beach it was just Jess, and the sea gulls, and the misty rain.

Jess just sat there. On the outside she felt the cool wet mist in her face. On the inside, she felt numb. She still couldn't believe what Reed Petersen had done to her.

A lone figure appeared down the beach, walking slowly toward her. As it got closer, Jess could see it was one of the town employees, wearing an olive-green poncho and dragging a garbage bag as he picked up trash and litter with a pointed stick. What a great job, Jess thought with a smirk.

As the figure approached her, he looked up. It was Billy.

"Great day, huh?" he said with a slight smile as he stopped beside the chair and stared out at the waves.

"Yeah, really," Jess said.

"Well, I guess I'm lucky I didn't get into trouble in the winter," Billy said. "Imagine having to collect litter in the snow. Now that would be a real bummer."

Jess smiled. Billy had really changed. No longer was he a loud showoff with a hungry eye for every female shape. Ever since he'd gotten in trouble he'd become quiet and polite. It seemed as if he'd really learned a lesson.

"Find anything good today?" Jess asked.

Billy rolled his eyes. "The Skittles bags have been running pretty strong for the last couple of days. Last week I had a pretty good run on Häagen-Dazs ice cream wrappers."

"Sounds like it has something to do with the weather," Jess guessed.

"Probably." Billy nodded.

The wind picked up and the drizzle turned into rain. Jess pulled the hood of the rain suit low over her eyes to keep the drops off her face. It was funny how the day reflected her mood. She felt lost and alone. With Reed, her life had been so bright and full of colors. Now it was a dreary gray wasteland.

Standing at the base of the chair, Billy turned his back to the rain. Here they were, two outcasts, Jess thought.

"Jess?" someone called.

Jess looked to her left and saw Hank coming toward her in a yellow rain suit. He stopped a few feet from the chair.

"The forecast is for more rain," Hank said. "No one's going to come to the beach today. I'm letting everyone go." He turned to Billy. "Billy, your supervisor just called. He said if I saw you I should tell you to knock off for the rest of the day."

"Thanks, Hank," Billy said.

Hank headed back toward the lifeguard shack. Jess climbed out of the chair and walked with Billy back up the beach. Billy was quiet. But when they reached the parking lot, he turned to her.

"Need a ride home?"

"Okay, thanks," Jess said.

They walked over to Billy's jeep and got in. A few moments later they were driving down the beach road. As Jess stared out through the rain-covered windshield, she realized she wasn't looking forward to another day alone in her room.

But Andy would probably be with Lisa.

And she told herself she didn't care where Reed was.

"Do you want to take a ride, Billy?" she asked. "Like we did the other day?"

"Today?" Billy looked surprised. "I guess we could, but there won't be a lot to see."

Jess knew he was right. With the rain and mist it was hardly a day for sightseeing.

"You want to go down to my dad's boat?" Billy asked.

"What would we do there?" Jess asked.

"I don't know," Billy said. "We could hang

around, watch TV. The kitchen's usually pretty well stocked."

Jess had an idea. "Does he have any cards?"

"You mean, like playing cards?" Billy asked. "Sure."

"Do you like to play gin rummy?" Jess asked.

"Oh, yeah," Billy said. "We could do that."

ELEVEN

Reed and Paula wound up going to the movies. It had been Reed's idea, actually. He'd been so shaken by Jess's behavior that he just didn't feel like being alone. Besides, it was obvious Paula was making a real effort to be nice. For the first time in a long time, Reed didn't mind being with her.

They got to the movie house early and bought popcorn and Cokes and then went inside. The theater was almost empty and they took seats about two-thirds of the way to the screen. The next closest person was nearly ten rows back.

"Remember how we always used to go to movies in the city?" Paula asked wistfully as they munched on popcorn and stared at the blank white screen while waiting for the previews to begin. "We'd go out to dinner at ten and catch a midnight show. And sometimes we'd even go out to a party after that?"

"Yes." Reed remembered. They hadn't done it that often, but it had been sort of a kick to wander around the city at all hours of the night and sometimes not get home until dawn.

"Don't you ever feel like doing that anymore?" Paula asked.

"Not really," Reed answered truthfully. "I mean, it was fun for a while. But how many times do you have to stay up all night before it starts to wear a little thin?"

"I just remember how exciting it was," Paula said with a sigh. "I don't feel like anything exciting's happened lately."

Reed turned and stared at her, surprised.

"What is it, Reed?"

"Didn't I have to fish you out of the harbor a couple of days ago?" he asked with a smile. "That seemed pretty exciting to me."

Paula bit her lip. She'd forgotten about that little "incident." But it was too late. Reed was now studying her with a skeptical look on his face.

"Don't tell me you've already forgotten about that," he said.

"Well . . ." Paula quickly glanced around, looking for something to distract Reed with. But all she saw were empty seats.

"Paula?" Reed pressed her for an answer.

"Huh?" Paula tried to play dumb.

"I know you couldn't have forgotten about that," Reed said.

Paula knew Reed wasn't going to let it drop. "I didn't jump off any boat," she admitted.

"What about the college guys who picked you up at the Salty Dog?" Reed asked.

"There were no college guys," Paula said. "I just wanted to get your attention."

Reed slumped back in his seat. "Why aren't I surprised to hear that?" he asked with a knowing smile.

"Can you blame me?" Paula asked. "I mean, I knew you were going to a party with Jess and all your lifeguarding friends. Meanwhile I was doing nothing."

"So it was all staged," Reed said.

"Yes, but wait," Paula said. "I know that you're thinking it was just Paula up to her old tricks again, but it really wasn't, Reed."

"Oh?" Reed raised a skeptical eyebrow. "Then what was it?"

"It was me trying to get your attention," Paula said. "Not for selfish or self-serving reasons. Not because I wanted to show you off to my friends. Not because I wanted you for status. But because I really care about you, Reed. I mean, I keep trying to show you how I've changed, but the biggest change is that I realized that I really, really care for you."

She leaned over and took his hand in hers. "I just want us to get back together, Reed. I'll do anything to make that happen."

Reed gazed back at her and held her eyes with his. "You don't have to throw yourself in the harbor and make up crazy stories."

"Then tell me what I do have to do," Paula said.

"I don't know," Reed said with a sigh. "I'm just not sure about anything anymore."

Reed turned and looked again at the screen. Paula just sat there holding his hand in hers and staring at his profile.

"You know what I really wish?" she said softly. "I wish summer was over and we were back at school."

Reed understood what she meant. It had been a very strange summer . . . filled with extremes. During the times when he'd been with Jess he'd wished the summer could last forever. But then there were times like now when he, too, couldn't wait for the summer to end.

"Well, I guess it'll be over soon enough," he said.

Paula turned to him. "Why wait?" she asked.

"Huh?" Reed frowned. "What do you mean?"

"There are only a few weeks left," Paula said. "We could go away for the rest of the summer. I mean, now that you and Jess have broken up, there's really no reason for you to stick around. We could go to Greece or Spain or even out West."

Reed froze. It was one thing to go to lunch and a movie with an old girlfriend, but to go to Europe with one was a different story. And something else was bothering him. How did Paula know he and Jess had broken up?

Paula must have seen that his reaction wasn't instantly positive. "Really, Reed, I mean, haven't you taken this lifeguarding thing far enough? I know you feel seriously about your obligation to the town, but that doesn't mean you have to be a slave to it. Why don't we go away? Why don't we go have some fun?"

Reed gazed back at her blankly. Who actually knew that he and Jess had broken up? Lisa, Andy, and Jess, by his count. Reed doubted any of them would have told Paula.

Then how did Paula know?

"Reed?" Paula said.

Reed knew she wanted an answer as far as going away was concerned. But right now he didn't want to give her one. He couldn't let on that he was starting to suspect something wasn't right.

How did Paula know?

Fortunately, just then the movie started to play.

Jess sat on the plush-carpeted floor in the cabin cruiser with her back against the couch. She and Billy were playing gin rummy. It was nice and warm because Billy had turned on the electric heater. There was music to listen to and snacks to munch on. Once again Jess felt free and at ease. No one knew where she was. No one could find her. Sitting there in the boat she could almost pretend the rest of the world didn't exist.

Billy sat across from her, pretending to play cards, but feeling very distracted. He'd always been aware of how beautiful Jess was, but now he was starting to see just why his brother had been so attracted to her. There was something about Jess that just made Billy feel good when he was with her. He'd been acutely aware of it the evening they'd taken their long drive together, but he knew if he made any demands on her he'd lose her.

He didn't want to lose her. . . .

"Gin," Jess said, laying down her cards. She put her hand over her mouth and yawned.

"You tired?" Billy asked as he gave her his cards so she could add up the score.

Jess nodded. "I haven't been sleeping well. And it's so warm and cozy here." She glanced at her watch.

"You have to go?" Billy asked.

"Not yet," Jess said. "In a little while."

Billy didn't want her to go. He got up. "Want something to drink?"

"You don't have a Coke, do you?" Jess asked.

"I'll go see." Billy got up and went down to the galley. Opening the refrigerator, he found that it was filled with beer and soda. Probably left over from that party Reed had. Suddenly Billy had an idea. "Uh, how about Cherry Coke?" he called back to Jess.

"That's fine," Jess said.

"I'll get it for you in a second," Billy said. "I just have to go below for a moment."

Billy went down the steps toward the stateroom, but made a left into the bathroom. Opening the medicine chest he found a bottle of cherry-flavored cough syrup. A moment later he went back up to the galley.

"One Cherry Coke coming up," he said. Keeping his back to Jess, he poured several tablespoons of syrup into a glass filled with regular Coke, and then returned to the living room.

"Here you go," he said, handing her the glass.

Jess took a gulp and then frowned. "Tastes a little mediciney," she said.

"Maybe it's the can," Billy said as he picked up the cards. "So what's the score?"

"I'm ahead forty-three to thirty-one," Jess said.

"What do you say we play to one hundred?" Billy said.

It wasn't long before Jess began to feel sleepy. It was probably because she'd been sleeping so poorly lately. That, plus the fact that the cabin cruiser was warm and rocking slightly began to make it hard for her to keep her eyes open. Suddenly she felt her eyelids droop.

"You really *are* tired," Billy said.

"Yes." She could hardly keep her eyes open.

"Why don't you lie down on the couch and take a nap?"

Jess nodded and stretched out on the couch, resting her head on one of the pillows. A few moments later she was asleep.

Billy stood up and went down into the stateroom. He came back with an afghan. He gently laid it over her and then took a step back and

gazed down in wonder. Jess Sloat lay before him
with her eyes closed and her long blonde hair
spread out on the pillow. Her lips were parted
slightly, and she was taking light slow breaths.
Billy felt almost mesmerized. Here was the most
beautiful girl in Far Hampton, lying on his
couch, asleep. She was his, finally. But what
would he do with her?

Billy had an idea. He went out on the deck
and unfastened the lines to the dock. Then he
went back inside and took the boat's wheel. He
had decided to go to sea.

Halfway through the movie Reed realized
there was one other person who knew he was
no longer seeing Jess: Billy. His brother had
asked him about it just the other night. At the
time, Reed hadn't thought much of it. But if
Paula had learned about Jess from Billy, then
Reed had reason to think something fishy was
going on. The only times Billy and Paula spoke
to each other was when they were cooking up
some kind of scheme.

Or maybe Reed was just being paranoid.

The movie ended.

"Feel like getting some ice cream?" Paula
asked.

"Uh, thanks, but no thanks," Reed said. Jess had spoken about that tape. A tape of Reed and Lisa.

Billy . . . Paula . . . videotape . . .

No, it couldn't be. . . .

Billy had been acting so low key lately. Reed should have known something was going on.

As they stepped back out into the lobby of the movie theater, Reed noticed that it had started to rain harder.

"So what do you want to do?" Paula asked.

"I think I'd better head home," Reed said. "Think you could give me a ride back to my jeep?"

"Are you sure that's what you want to do?" Paula asked.

Reed nodded. He had to figure this out.

They ran back through the rain to Paula's car and got in. Paula started to drive back to the beach.

"I guess the idea of going away with me isn't that appealing," Paula said.

"It's not that," Reed replied, not wanting to let her know what he was thinking. "But you were right before. I do feel an obligation to my job. I think I should stick with it until the end."

"Do you really believe that people look at you

and think, 'Thank God Reed Petersen is a lifeguard even though he doesn't have to be'?" Paula
asked.

"It doesn't matter, Paula," Reed replied. "I
grew up spending my summers out here and
now I want to give something back."

Paula nodded and stared out through the
windshield at the wet road. Now it was Reed's
turn to ask a question.

"Tell me something, Paula," he said. "Remember that night I came home and you were
at the house?"

Paula glanced at him. "Yes?"

"You said you'd been there to talk to Billy
about something personal," Reed said. "Mind if
I ask what that was?"

"Why do you want to know?" Paula asked.

"I'm just curious, that's all," Reed said.

"Well . . ." Paula paused. "I went to see him
about you."

"Me?" Reed asked, surprised. "What would
Billy know about me?"

"I was hoping he'd know whether you really
hated me or not," Paula lied.

"And what did he say?"

"He said he didn't know," Paula replied.

"And that was it?" Reed guessed.

"Basically."

It was funny how, when you knew someone long enough, you almost developed a second sense of when they were lying. Reed had that feeling now. Maybe he was crazy, but he had this picture of Billy and Paula plotting to put crazy ideas in Jess's head. Ideas that would drive her away from Reed.

They got to the beach. The parking lot was awash with rainwater. Only two cars were left: Reed's jeep and Hank's van. Reed realized that because of the weather, Hank must have sent the rest of the lifeguards home.

Paula pulled up next to the jeep.

"Thanks for lunch and the movie," Reed said and started to push open the car door.

"Reed, wait." Paula reached across the seat and took his arm.

Reed gazed back at her. "What, Paula?"

"I . . . I told you I still care about you," Paula said. "Doesn't that mean anything?"

Reed nodded. "Is Billy up to something?"

Paula looked surprised. "Like what?"

She seemed genuinely surprised that he'd asked. Reed wondered if he'd been imagining things after all. "I don't know," he said.

Paula still hadn't let go of his arm. "What about us, Reed?"

"I don't know, Paula."

Paula turned and stared away into the rain.

"I'm sorry, Paula," Reed said and got out.

He decided to go in and say hello to Hank before he went home. He found the lifeguard captain inside the shack, watching the weather on the radar. A small electric heater was on.

"Hey, Reed," Hank said, looking up from the radar.

"How's it look?" Reed asked.

Hank pointed at a light green splotch in the middle of the dark green screen. "Looks like a storm coming in."

"I see you sent the rest of the crew home," Reed said, staring out the window at the broad empty beach.

"Wasn't much sense in keeping them," Hank said. "Now that Gary's gone, no one in their right mind would want to come out to the beach on a day like this."

The mention of Gary's name made Reed think of Jess again. "Jess take the bus home?" he asked.

"Don't know," Hank said. "Last I saw, she was walking out toward the parking lot with your brother."

Reed blinked. "Are you sure, Hank?"

"Yup." The lifeguard captain nodded.

"Uh, thanks," Reed said, going back into the rain. "See you later."

He got into his jeep and started to drive home. Why in the world would Jess go anywhere with Billy? The last time she'd done that he'd practically attacked her.

Reed got home and went up to his room and called Jess's house. Mrs. Sloat answered and Reed asked her if she'd seen Jess. Mrs. Sloat said she hadn't seen Jess since she'd left for work that morning. Reed asked Mrs. Sloat to have Jess call him as soon as she got in. He told her it was very important.

Reed hung up the phone and stared out the window. The sky was gray and the wind had picked up, capping the ocean waves with white.

Where was Jess? Where was Billy?

Reed got up and walked down the hall to Billy's room. He stepped inside and looked around. The room was a mess — tapes and CDs everywhere.

What if Billy had made a tape?

Reed shook his head. Naw, he was imagining things. Billy had learned his lesson after the radar incident. He couldn't be stupid enough to try something like that again.

But wait, this was Billy he was thinking about.

Reed looked around the room and shook his head. It would take forever to go through all these tapes. And he wasn't even certain what he was looking for. Still, until he heard that Jess was home, he was going to try.

Keeping one hand on the cabin cruiser's wheel, Billy cracked open his fourth Budweiser and took a big gulp. It was mighty nice that Reed had left the boat's fridge filled with soft drinks and beer. The cabin cruiser rocked up and down. The wind had picked up and the waves had gotten bigger, but Billy wasn't worried. This was a big boat and it would stand up to just about anything.

Behind him on the couch Jess stirred and opened her eyes. She felt woozy and heavy-headed and it took her a moment to realize she was in the boat and that it was rocking up and down as if it were out on the ocean. Jess looked out the window and realized they *were* out on the ocean. Then she saw Billy sitting at the wheel with his back toward her.

She sat up, feeling dizzy. "Billy?"

Billy turned and smiled at her. "Sleep well?"

"Yes, but what's going on? Where are we going?"

"I just felt like taking the boat out," Billy said.

As Jess's eyes focused more she saw several empty red-and-white beer cans on the floor around Billy's seat. She realized he was holding another one in his hand.

"Billy," she said, suddenly apprehensive. "I want to go back."

"We will," Billy replied.

"I meant now," Jess said.

But Billy shook his head. "Not yet."

Jess's apprehension was quickly becoming fear. She looked around, but out the windows all she could see was rough water in every direction.

What was he going to do with her?

"Billy, I really mean it," she said. "I want you to take me back right now."

In the captain's seat, Billy didn't answer. He was busy turning the wheel and pressing some levers.

"Did you hear me?" Jess asked behind him.

Billy nodded and slid out of the chair to face her. He took a gulp from his beer. "You know what's great about this boat?" he said, ignoring her question. "You press a button and the anchor goes down. You press it again and it comes back up. No one has to go out in the rain and get wet trying to pull the stupid anchor up."

"Where are we?" Jess asked.

"Not far from the harbor," Billy said, gazing out the back of the boat. "Maybe half a mile."

Jess turned and saw something she'd missed before — a thin strip of land off the stern. It must have been Far Hampton. She turned back to Billy.

"What are we doing out here?" she asked.

"I thought maybe we'd talk," Billy said, stepping toward her.

"Why couldn't we have talked back in the harbor?" Jess asked.

"I don't know," Billy said. "I guess I felt like talking out here."

He was coming closer. Jess glanced around, looking for something, anything, to protect herself with. Suddenly Billy stopped a few feet from her and sat down in a chair opposite the couch.

"You look scared, Jess," he said. "Don't be scared. I won't hurt you."

"You've been drinking," Jess said.

Billy held up the can of beer and stared at it. Then turned to her and nodded with a slight smile. "Yeah."

"Why?" Jess asked.

"I don't know. Guess I felt a little nervous."

"About what?"

Billy shrugged. "Being out here with you."

"Then maybe we ought to go back and you won't have to feel nervous anymore," Jess said.

Billy's expression changed. He looked serious.

"I told you, you have nothing to be scared of."

"But you understand why I might be feeling that way," Jess said. "I mean, last time . . ."

"I told you I've changed," Billy snapped, suddenly angry.

Jess stared back at him and didn't reply. Yes, he said he'd changed. And part of that change was not drinking anymore. But if anything, he was acting more like the old Billy than ever.

TWELVE

Reed had fast-forwarded through a dozen tapes and a thousand images. It had gotten hard to focus his eyes, and he'd begun to wonder if he were wasting his time. If Jess had a tape, why did it have to come from Billy? And why did Reed assume there would be a copy here?

He was probably wasting his time.

And yet he couldn't stop. The thought of Jess kept him going.

He'd just finished one tape and now slid another in. As it started to play, he stood up and stretched. Behind him, a blurred gray scene appeared on the monitor. Reed glanced at it and shook his head. He could hardly tell what it was. He was starting to turn away again when he saw something out of the corner of his eye that caught his attention. A face had appeared on the video.

Reed turned back and stared. The picture was

blurred and fuzzy and obviously taken in bad light. The face looked like Paula's, but instead of having wavy blow-dried hair, it was straight, like Lisa's. Now she moved away from the camera, turning her back toward it. She seemed to be wearing a jacket with something on the back.

Reed stepped toward the table and took a closer look.

A rose!

It was Lisa's denim jacket. And the room looked familiar. Like the stateroom in the cabin cruiser. Paula sat down on the bunk with her back to the camera and Reed realized that from that angle, there was no way anyone could know it was Paula and not Lisa.

Then Reed watched as he entered the stateroom and stood by the bunk opposite Paula. He knew now what he was watching. It was the day he'd pulled Paula out of the harbor. The day she'd made up that story about those guys on the boat. Reed watched as they talked. Then Paula reached up and pulled him toward her. Reed remembered how she'd been crying and he'd put his arms around her to comfort her.

As he watched it all being replayed on the monitor he realized it had been a setup with Paula pretending to be Lisa. *This* was what Jess must have seen.

Reed turned off the monitor and called Jess's house again. Mrs. Sloat said Jess still hadn't come home. Reed hung up and called Lisa's house.

"Hello?" Lisa answered.

"It's Reed. Do you have any idea where Jess is?"

"Uh, no. Why?"

"It's a long story," Reed said. "Do you think Andy might know?"

"No, but he's here so let me ask him." She got off the phone.

"He doesn't know," Lisa said, getting back on the phone. "What's going on?"

Reed quickly explained about the tape.

"So *that's* what Jess saw," Lisa gasped.

"Billy must have been trying to convince Jess that we were all against her," Reed said. "Then he figured he'd move in."

"And you think Jess is with Billy right now?" Lisa asked.

"I'd bet on it," Reed said. "Hank said he saw them leave the beach together."

"You don't think he'd do anything to her, do you?" Lisa asked.

"After what he did last time, I don't know what to think," Reed said. "All I know is I want to find her fast."

"Andy and I will help," Lisa said. "Just tell us what to do."

"Go into town and ask if anyone's seen them," Reed said. "And try the Crab Shack and anyplace else they might go. I'll meet you at the lifeguard shack in forty-five minutes."

"What are you going to do?" Lisa asked.

"I'm going to see Paula," Reed said.

It took ten minutes to get to Paula's. Paula's parents owned a large whitewashed contemporary house on the bay. Reed drove his jeep up the driveway and found a limousine parked in front of the house. A driver in a black uniform was putting several suitcases in the trunk. Reed parked the jeep and hopped out into the rain.

"Is Paula around?" he asked.

"Inside," the driver said.

Reed turned toward the house, but before he could reach the front door, Paula came out wearing a white raincoat and rain hat. She was carrying a travel bag. She looked very surprised to see him.

"What are you doing here?" she asked.

"You're going?" Reed asked.

"Don't tell me you've suddenly decided to care," Paula replied.

"Did you know about the tape?" Reed asked.

"I . . . I . . ." Paula shook her head. "No, I don't know what you're talking about."

"Don't lie to me, Paula," Reed said angrily.

"Why do you think I'm lying?" Paula asked.

"Because I saw the tape," Reed said. "And you knew Jess and I had broken up. The only people who knew about that were Andy, Lisa, and Billy. Andy and Lisa didn't tell you. That means Billy did."

"So?" Paula said.

"So the reason you jumped into the harbor was so that we'd let you on the boat and give you Lisa's clothes to wear," Reed said. "Billy must've planted the camera in the stateroom. The whole idea was for you to put Lisa's jacket on and get me into the stateroom."

Paula stared down at the puddles in the driveway. "He made me do it, Reed."

"He *made* you? How?"

"It's not important," Paula said. "But believe me, he did." She pressed her hands against her eyes and started to cry.

"Did you know he was going to give the tape to Jess?" Reed asked.

Paula shook her head.

"Do you have any idea where Billy is right now?"

Again Paula shook her head.

"Listen, Paula, it's important," Reed said. "Jess could be in danger. For God's sake tell me."

"I swear I don't know," Paula said, wiping the tears from her eyes.

Reed believed her. He turned back toward the jeep.

"Reed, wait!" Paula cried.

Reed stopped and stared back at her, standing in the rain in her white raincoat, with rainwater dripping off the brim of her white rain hat. "What, Paula?"

Paula came toward him, her eyes red-rimmed. "I know you must hate me, but there's one thing you have to believe. I really, really love you."

Reed could feel the rain matting down his hair and seeping through his shirt. "I believe you, Paula. But you sure have a strange way of showing it."

Billy sat across from Jess and took another gulp of beer. Jess remained standing behind the couch, watching him.

"Have a seat, Jess," Billy said.

Jess crossed her arms tightly before her. "No, thanks. I think I'll stand."

Billy just stared at her for a moment. "Jeez, Jess, why do you have to be like this?"

"Because you're holding me against my will," Jess said.

"Is that how you see it?" Billy asked, looking a little hurt. "I'm *holding* you here?"

"Is there any other way to see it?" Jess asked.

Billy cupped his hands around the beer can and looked at her earnestly. "I thought we were friends. I thought we had something in common."

Jess was tempted to ask him what in the world he thought they had in common, but she had to be careful not to antagonize him. Instead, she sat down on the couch and leaned toward him.

"You're right, Billy," she said. "I do feel like you're my friend. And that's why I'm asking you to take me back to the harbor. If you're my friend, you'd do that."

Billy tipped up the beer can and drained it. Then he put the can down and shook his head. "You don't believe me."

"Believe what, Billy?" Jess asked.

"That I won't hurt you," Billy said. "I told you I wouldn't. I just want to be with you. Is that so bad?"

Jess knew better than to suggest again that he could just as easily be with her back in the harbor. It would only make him mad. "No, it's not so bad," she said. "In fact, I guess I'm a little flattered."

Billy stared at her and she couldn't read his expression. "I think we have a lot in common," he said. "We've both been stabbed in the back by my brother."

Jess was tempted to ask how Billy felt Reed had betrayed him, but then something else occurred to her. How did Billy know Reed had done anything to *her*? The one time they'd talked about Reed, Jess had implied that she hadn't gotten back together with him after Gary drowned. Unless Reed said something to him.

The cabin cruiser rocked in the waves, and Jess listened to the patter of the rain against the windows. She couldn't help wondering how long Billy would keep her there.

"Don't you want to get back at him?" Billy asked.

Jess shook her head. It might have been odd, but she didn't. Even though he'd used her and she felt terribly hurt, it had never occurred to her to want revenge.

"Is that why you brought me out here?" she asked. "Is this some kind of revenge against Reed?"

"Last time it was," Billy said.

"And this time?" Jess asked.

Billy just shrugged shyly. Jess felt more uncomfortable. He still hadn't explained why they were out here in this rough weather. Now he leaned forward in the chair, looking very earnest.

"Jess, I know I did something pretty bad to you out on the point," he said. "But you know I was mad because you were secretly trying to tape me, right?"

Jess nodded.

"But since then we've had some pretty nice times together," Billy said. "I mean, I know we haven't spent a lot of time together, but I felt like you were comfortable with me at least."

"Yes," Jess said.

"I mean, we had fun that day we drove around," Billy said.

Jess nodded. She wasn't certain she'd describe it as fun, but she wasn't about to argue. Across from her, Billy stood up. He seemed a little unsteady as he took a step toward her.

Jess quickly got up from the couch.

"Where are you going?" Billy asked.

"I, uh, just felt like standing," Jess replied.

"No, you didn't." Billy's face darkened. "You're still afraid of me."

"No, Billy, it's not that," Jess said nervously.

"Don't *lie* to me," Billy said angrily. The boat heaved again and in his drunken state he had to hold onto the edge of a table to keep from losing his balance. "After what we've been through I don't deserve that."

"After what *we've* been through?" Jess repeated. "I'm not sure I know what you're talking about."

Billy took another step toward her. "That evening we spent together."

"It was just an evening, Billy," Jess replied, backing behind the couch. "I don't mean to hurt you, but it didn't change my life."

"Don't say that," Billy said. "It was more than that for both of us."

Jess didn't know what he was talking about. Meanwhile, Billy took another step toward her.

"You never meant anything to my brother," Billy said. "You were just a good-looking babe he could use to show off to everyone on the beach. Believe me, Jess. To him you're just another score, just another trophy on his shelf."

"I believe you, Billy," Jess said.

"But that evening we spent together just driving around and jumping off the cliffs, I felt something," Billy said. "We could be together without proving anything to each other. It was just you and me, Jess. That was all it had to be. Didn't you feel that, too?"

Jess remembered the evening well. All she'd felt was the pain of knowing Reed had used her, and that Lisa had gone after Reed and Andy. Billy had just been someone to be with so she wouldn't have to be alone. He'd been the only one left.

"Didn't you feel it, Jess?" Billy asked again. He'd reached the couch now. Jess took another step back and felt herself bump into the sliding glass door that led to the rear deck. Meanwhile, Billy was coming around the couch toward her.

"I . . . I feel like you're my friend, Billy," Jess stammered.

Billy stopped. He was only a few feet from her now and there was nothing between them. Jess felt the sliding door against her back.

"I don't want to be your *friend*," he said.

Lisa's VW and Hank's van were the only cars in the rain-swept parking lot when Reed got there. Both were empty, so Reed parked his jeep and went into the lifeguard shack. Inside, he found Hank watching the radar. Lisa and Andy stood nearby with anxious looks on their faces.

"Any sign of her?" Lisa asked as soon as Reed came in.

Reed shook his head. "How about you?"

Lisa and Andy shook their heads.

"We looked everywhere," Lisa said. "All the places in town, the movie theater, everywhere."

"No sign of them or Billy's jeep," Andy added.

Reed stared silently out the window of the lifeguard shack at the rough gray waves crashing on the beach.

"You know, it's possible that they just went for a drive," Hank said. "I saw Jess get into Billy's jeep. It wasn't like he had to drag her into it."

"Did Lisa and Andy tell you about the tape?" Reed asked.

"Yes, but it still doesn't mean that Jess is in any kind of danger," Hank said.

"You might be right, Hank," Reed said. "Then again, you might not."

"You've looked everywhere in town," Hank said. "What else can you do?"

"Call the police?" Lisa suggested.

"Believe me, they'll tell you there's no reason to think Jess is in any trouble," Hank said.

Reed gave him a sharp look.

"Hey," Hank said. "I'm not saying you're wrong, Reed. I'm just telling you that's what the police will say. Even Chief Sloat would need more to go on."

Reed nodded. He knew Hank was right.

"So what do we do now?" Andy asked.

Reed didn't know. If Billy and Jess weren't in town, they could be anywhere. The only thing Reed and the others could do would be to wait and see what happened. But if Billy was up to something, by the time they found him it might be too late.

"Hold it," Lisa said, turning to Reed. "There is one place we haven't looked — your father's boat."

"You're right," Reed said. He started to turn toward the door.

"Wait, Reed," Hank said. "I don't know what this'll mean, but about two hours ago I saw something that looked like a cabin cruiser on the radar. It left the harbor and then anchored about half a mile due south. It seemed like a pretty strange thing to do in this kind of weather."

"Okay," Reed said to Andy and Lisa. "You guys go down to the harbor. I'm going back to my house. Call me when you get there and tell me if the *Gaila*'s in her berth."

"And if it isn't?" Andy asked.

"I'll take my sailboat and go get her," Reed said.

Hank looked surprised. "You're going to go try to find her in this?" he asked, pointing out the window at the pouring rain and rough waves.

"You're damn straight," Reed said, heading for the door.

"That," Hank said behind him, "is true love."

THIRTEEN

"Stop, Billy!" Jess cried out. Billy had backed her into a corner, and was reaching toward her.

"Come on, Jess," Billy growled.

"Get away from me or I'll really hurt you," she warned.

But Billy only seemed amused. "Aw, give it up, Jess."

Jess shoved him away and quickly darted around the couch. "Now please take me back to the harbor."

But Billy just glared at her.

"Billy?" she said uncertainly.

He staggered toward her. "I'm not going to hurt you."

"Billy, *why* won't you let me go?" Jess gasped.

Billy didn't answer. He came closer, staring at her with a strange look on his face. Jess backed against the sliding glass door. She could hear the wind whistling and the loud patter of rain splashing on the deck and the roof of the cabin. The boat rocked again in the rain, and Billy stumbled against a chair and then regained his balance.

"Please, Billy," Jess said.

But Billy just took another step closer. Jess could feel her heart pounding in her chest. Her breaths were short, and her throat felt tight.

"Billy, please . . ." she begged.

But Billy just stared at her.

Reed picked up the phone before the first ring was finished. Andy was on the other end of the line.

"The *Gaila*'s not there," he said.

"Okay, thanks." Reed started to hang up.

"Reed, wait," Andy said. "You sure you want to go out there in this weather?"

Reed stared out the window of his room. The wind had picked up and the waves had grown bigger and rougher-looking.

"Yes," he said.

"Well, good luck," Andy said.

"What are you going to do, Billy?" Jess asked nervously.

Billy didn't answer. Jess knew she had to find some way to talk him out of this.

"Is this some kind of competition with Reed?" she asked.

Billy scowled. "What are you talking about?"

"He has to have four girls this summer so you think you do, too," Jess said.

"Yeah, that's it," Billy said with a leering smile.

But Jess sensed that wasn't it at all. "Billy, why are you doing this?"

"You really have to ask?" Billy replied.

"You'll go to jail," Jess said.

"For what?" Billy asked, feigning innocence.

"For what I think you plan to do."

"What do I plan to do?" Billy asked.

Jess felt a sickening sensation in the pit of her stomach. He was toying with her, teasing her.

"Billy, please take me back in," Jess begged.

But Billy only stepped closer. "No way, Jess."

It was crazy to go out in weather like this. Reed sailed with the small jib sail only. It was far too rough and windy to use the mainsail. *Simplicity* bucked and heaved through the waves as he struggled with the rudder to keep her on course. In the rain and wind he only had a few hundred yards visibility. But according to the compass he was headed in the right direction.

Simplicity made slow progress through the

rough waters. The crashing waves and ocean swells kept throwing the sailboat off course. At least once a minute a wave would crash over the side and drench Reed with cold seawater. The driving rain blurred Reed's vision as he clung to the rudder, fighting to keep her on course.

Suddenly a big wave crashed right over the cockpit, knocking the rudder out of his hands.

The next thing Reed knew, he was thrown overboard into the cold, surging water.

Jess glanced around, desperately looking for a way out. The boat kept rocking and both she and Billy had to hold on to keep from falling.

"Come on, Jess," Billy said, stepping even closer.

Jess pressed her back against the cold glass sliding door. She could feel the latch pressing against her. She glanced back through the glass at the rain-slickened deck. What good would it do to go out there?

Billy stepped closer. Jess didn't know what he was going to do. She stopped breathing for a moment. She could feel the pulse of each heart-beat through her fingertips. He reached forward to grab her.

Jess felt herself take a sharp breath. Trembling, she reached up to push his hand away.

"Take your hands away," he hissed, reaching toward the collar of her blouse.

Reed hung from *Simplicity*'s railing by one hand. His body was half submerged in the swirling waters beside the sailboat. Without someone to man the rudder, *Simplicity* pitched and rocked helplessly in the waves.

Suddenly the sailboat tipped in the trough between two large waves and Reed went under completely.

But he held on and gradually worked his other hand up to the railing. Tired, drenched, and cold, he managed to pull himself back into the sailboat and took over the rudder again.

But the storm had blown him off course. All he could see was gray rain and waves in every direction. Where was the *Gaila*?

Billy's fingers were inches from her throat. Jess could feel her heart racing. It was beating so hard she thought it might explode. She was so terrified she could hardly breathe.

She had to do something.

The latch to the sliding door was pressing into her back.

Billy's fingers were coming closer.

"Wait, Billy," she whispered. "Let me."

Billy straightened up and smiled.

Jess reached behind herself . . . and undid the door latch. In a flash she slid open the glass door and stepped backward onto the rain-soaked deck. The cold rain caused goose bumps to run up and down her arms as Jess looked around for something to protect herself with.

Except for some white seat cushions, the deck was bare.

Billy followed her out into the rain. Jess quickly picked up one of the seat cushions and covered herself with it as she backed toward the stern.

Billy stepped toward her with a smile on his face. "What's the point, Jess?"

The boat rocked up and down in the waves. Billy grabbed a gunwale to support himself, but he kept inching closer. Jess backed into a corner. The spray of crashing waves splashed over her, and she hugged the cushion tightly.

There was no escape.

Jess looked around desperately. Suddenly her eyes fixed on some small black print on the seat cushion indicating it could be used as a flotation device.

Jess quickly turned and looked back toward Far Hampton harbor. It was barely visible in the driving rain and wind-blown spray.

It had to be at least half a mile away with nothing but big, rough waves in between.

Could she make it?

Billy was only a few feet away now.

Jess climbed over the stern and jumped.

The water was cold and turbulent. Clutching the cushion tightly, Jess bobbed up and down in the waves a dozen feet from the boat. Billy leaned over the side and stared at her with a crazy look on his face.

A big wave crashed over Jess, submerging her for a few moments, but the cushion quickly brought her back to the surface. When she came back up, Billy was no longer watching her from the back of the boat.

What was he going to do now?

Sitting in *Simplicity,* his hair plastered down to his head, his clothes soaked, and his teeth chattering, Reed steered on. Ahead he thought he caught a glimpse of white through the rain and wind. He quickly changed his course and steered toward it.

Floating in the waves, Jess heard the *Gaila*'s engines turn over and start to chug. A white cloud of smoke puffed out the stern, and Jess caught a whiff of diesel exhaust. She heard a cranking sound and realized Billy was bringing up the anchor.

Now what?

She heard a rattle of chains as the anchor came up out of the water. The *Gaila*'s engines roared and the cabin cruiser plowed forward into the waves.

What was Billy doing? Was he going to try to catch her? Run her over?

Jess kept waiting for the boat to turn around toward her.

But it didn't.

Suddenly she realized what Billy was doing. He was leaving her there and sailing off into the storm.

Reed had just caught sight of the *Gaila* when he saw that she had started to move forward through the waves.

Damn, he thought. But he wasn't surprised. If he could see Billy, that meant Billy could see him. There was no way Reed was going to catch up to him now.

A big wave rocked *Simplicity*. The winds were getting stronger and the waves bigger. Reed had to decide what to do next. He could try to sail back to his dock at Breezes, or he could sail into

Far Hampton harbor and leave the sailboat there until the storm blew over.

He was probably closer to the harbor at this point. And the sooner he got in, the sooner he could alert the Coast Guard about Billy. Too bad his radio was still broken, or he could have called them faster.

Clutching the seat cushion, Jess was trying to kick through the waves toward shore when she caught sight of the sailboat off to her right. Who in the world? It had to be Reed!

"Reed!" she shouted, but a big wave curled over her and the sailboat disappeared from sight.

"Reed!" she cried again, but in the rain and wind and crashing of the waves she doubted he could hear her.

"Reed!" If he couldn't hear her, maybe he could see her. Jess let go of the cushion and waved with one arm.

Crash! She didn't see the wave that rose up and crashed over her. Suddenly Jess was underwater. The cushion was gone.

Reed turned *Simplicity* toward shore. He could see the *Gaila* motoring away in the distance. Billy had to be crazy to go out farther in this kind of weather. What was he going to do with Jess?

Jess swam to the surface and tried to tread water. *Simplicity* was only a hundred yards away now. It seemed like Reed had decided to sail in toward the harbor. In another few moments he'd be well past her.

"*Reed!*" she screamed.

Another wave crashed over her. Once again Jess had to struggle back to the surface. She was growing tired.

She fought back up to the surface and caught her breath. *Simplicity* was past her now and sailing toward shore.

"*Reed!*" Jess screamed again.

It sounded like a voice crying his name. In the cockpit of *Simplicity*, Reed turned and looked back into the waves and wind behind him. What was it? Could he have imagined it? He listened again, but all he heard was the whistle of the wind and the crash of the waves.

Struggling in the rough water, Jess watched *Simplicity* sail away, and with it, any hope of rescue.

"Reed!" she screamed one last time. But it seemed hopeless in the wind and crashing waves. Jess gasped for breath and curled into a ball, assuming the dead man's float. Wave after wave picked her up and dropped her. She had to try and conserve her energy if she was to have any chance of making it to shore. But her chances seemed dubious.

"Jess!"

In the water, Jess couldn't believe her ears. She looked up and saw the white jib of *Simplicity* coming back toward her.

"Here, Reed, here!" she cried, waving her arms.

Reed saw her now, just a dot in the waves yelling and waving. He had to tack the sailboat up against the wind, but soon he was close enough to throw her the life rope. Jess hooked her arms through it and he pulled her in.

"Here! Grab on!" Once he'd pulled her close to the sailboat, he leaned over and reached down. Jess grabbed his arms and he pulled her out of the water. Together they fell back into the cockpit in a soaking wet embrace.

"What happened?" Reed gasped, brushing the wet hair from her eyes. "What were you doing in the water?"

"Billy tried . . ." Jess shook her head. "It's too awful. It doesn't matter now."

"He made the tape, Jess," Reed panted. "He got Paula to wear Lisa's jacket. He made it look like I was with Lisa. But I swear, Jess, it wasn't what it looked like."

"He told me you wanted to have four girls this summer," Jess said, still gasping for breath.

Reed pressed his wet face against hers. "There's only one girl, Jess. You."

They made it back to the harbor and tied up in the *Gaila*'s berth. Inside *Simplicity*'s cabin, Reed made tea. They were both wrapped in dry blankets, their wet clothes in a heap on the floor.

"Here you go," Reed said, handing Jess a mug of steaming tea.

"What are you going to do about Billy?" Jess asked.

"I radioed the Coast Guard," Reed said. "They'll find him."

"I can't believe I didn't trust you," Jess said. "I'm sorry."

"That tape looked awful convincing," Reed said. "In that poor light and out of focus the way it was, you could never tell it was Paula and not Lisa."

"It didn't look like she had anything on under the jacket," Jess said.

"It was a setup," Reed said. "Billy edited it to look like we were being romantic."

"Will you forgive me for not believing you?" Jess asked.

"I'll do more than forgive you," Reed said. "I'll make sure you never have to doubt me again."

"How?" Jess asked.

Reed put down his mug and slid his fingers through her damp hair. "I'm not going back to St. Peter's this year. I'm staying here. I'll do my senior year at Far Hampton High. With you."

Then he leaned forward and kissed her.

She was in his arms again. Even while the wind outside blew and the rain splattered against the roof of *Simplicity*'s cabin, she felt safe and warm. Reed kissed her face, her ears, and her neck as he pressed against her.

"Promise me you'll always believe me," he whispered in her ear.

"I promise," she whispered, kissing his earlobe and running her fingers through his hair.

Reed held her tightly and she felt all his heat and passion. Finally, they were together again. And this time she would never let go.

*   *   *

There was a knock on the cabin door. Reed's eyes burst open. *Simplicity*'s cabin was dark. It must have been night. Jess lay asleep in his arms, her blonde hair spread out on his shoulders.

The knocking sound came again.

"Reed, you in there?" It was Andy's voice.

Now Jess stirred beside him and rubbed her eyes. "What is it, Reed?" she asked in a sleepy voice.

"Andy," Reed whispered back.

Beside him, Jess was quiet for a moment.

"We can pretend we're not here," Reed whispered. "That is, if you don't want him to know."

Jess looked up at him through the dark and kissed his lips lightly. "It's okay, Reed. I want everyone to know."

"Just a minute, Andy," Reed called. He sat up and lit the storm lanterns, then wrapped a blanket around himself and opened the cabin door. Andy and Lisa were outside.

"Watch your heads," Reed said.

Holding Lisa's hand, Andy ducked down and entered the cabin. He paused for a moment when he saw the pile of wet clothes on the floor and Jess on the bunk, covered by another blanket.

"You guys okay?" Andy asked, sitting down with Lisa on the bunk opposite Reed and Jess.

"Yes," Jess said, slipping her arm through Reed's. "Reed saved me."

Andy nodded. "I heard the Coast Guard contacted Hank. They found Billy. He's in really bad trouble."

Reed nodded grimly. Jess squeezed his arm tightly. Across from them, Lisa whispered something into Andy's ear. Andy nodded and cleared his throat.

"Reed, I, uh, owe you an apology," he said, extending his hand. "I guess I really had you pegged wrong."

"It's okay, Andy." Reed shook his hand and smiled. "You'll have all year to make it up to me."

"Huh?" Andy looked confused.

"He's staying here this year," Jess said happily.

"Really?" Lisa gasped, obviously thrilled for Jess.

Jess nodded happily and held Reed tightly.

Andy and Lisa went to get them some dry clothes. In the cabin of *Simplicity*, Jess snuggled against Reed's chest as the flames in the storm lanterns flickered. Reed had a faraway look in his eyes.

"Are you worried about Billy?" she asked.

Reed nodded. "Maybe something good will

come of this. They could put him in rehab. Maybe he'll finally get the kind of help he needs." He paused and looked back at Jess. "Let's not think about it now."

"What are you thinking about?" Jess asked.

"Being with you all year."

"Are you sure that you want to do it?" Jess asked. "I mean, Far Hampton High isn't exactly on the same level as St. Peter's Prep."

Reed looked down and kissed her gently on the lips. "Jess, I love you. I'd stay with you if it meant having to be the janitor."

Jess reached up and slid her arms around his neck, pulling him back down onto the bunk. "And I love you, Reed," she whispered, covering his face with kisses.

Don't miss out on the action!

Be sure to read *Lifeguards*

SUMMER'S PROMISE

Jess knows that this summer is going to be BIG. She's made it onto the Far Hampton lifeguard squad. For Jess, being a lifeguard is both dangerous *and* exciting — especially when it comes to Reed Petersen.

Reed's a lifeguard, too, and his family represents everything Jess despises. Jess has lived in Far Hampton for as long as she can remember, but Reed's family are summer people: rich, snobby, preppy, and cold. Yet Reed seems different. And Jess just can't get him out of her mind.

But Reed's girlfriend, Paula, gets whatever she wants. She's out to make sure Jess's relationship with Reed is *strictly* professional. And Billy, Reed's brother, is tired of seeing Reed get all the attention. When Paula and Billy get together, someone's sure to get hurt.

By midsummer, Jess's hopes may be shattered completely . . . and there's still more damage to be done. . . .